New Fiction

Upon The Shadows

Edited by

Sarah Marshall

First published in Great Britain in 2003 by
NEW FICTION
Remus House,
Coltsfoot Drive,
Peterborough, PE2 9JX
Telephone (01733) 898101
Fax (01733) 313524

All Rights Reserved

Copyright Contributors 2003

SB ISBN 1 85929 083 3

FOREWORD

When 'New Fiction' ceased publishing there was much wailing and gnashing of teeth, the showcase for the short story had offered an opportunity for practitioners of the craft to demonstrate their talent.

Phoenix-like from the ashes, 'New Fiction' has risen with the sole purpose of bringing forth new and exciting short stories from new and exciting writers.

The art of the short story writer has been practised from ancient days, with many gifted writers producing small, but hauntingly memorable stories that linger in the imagination.

I believe this selection of stories will leave echoes in your mind for many days. Read on and enjoy the pleasure of that most perfect form of literature, the short story.

Parvus Est Bellus.

CONTENTS

Here Is The News	Linda Rudden	1
Daddy's Little Girl	Mary Linney	4
Future Imperfect	Neil Campbell Roper	10
A Cruel Twist Of Fate	Liam Heaney	13
Quadrophenia 2: The Road To Nowhere	John Lee	21
The Second Thunder	David Russell	25
A Candid Story	Susan Booth	27
Anderson Joe - November 1940	F Lyndon	30
True Bill	Mary Cathleen Brown	40
Young Louis Has A Small Hangover In His Small World	Robert Creamer	44
Motorway Mike	Diana Stannus	53
Faraway Cottage	Ray Wilson	57
The Day My Ship Came In . . .	G K (Bill) Baker	59
Passing Through	Gardiner M Weir	62
Brambles	Robert D Shooter	66
Carol's Pandora's Box	Carol C Olson	68
Sleeping Partner	Jean Paisley	71
Aperture In Reality . . .	Cathy Stephens	74
Gypsy Blessing	M D Wyatt	77
If Only I Was A Millionaire	F R Smith	79
Keeping Up Apperances	Rosemary Pooley	84
The Colour Of Mozart	Jonathan Attrill	87
Horror Of Horrors	Ray Foxell	90
A Stormy Night	Claire Caple	95
Titanic In Ice	FAC	99
Colouring The Truth	Margaret Green	101

HERE IS THE NEWS
Linda Rudden

Here is the news:
Scientists have revealed that the continued high usage of mobile phones has resulted in the contamination of the British sheep population.

We now go live to the government chief audio scientist, Dr Sandra Gelling, for further information:

In the live link studio, Sandra swallowed nervously, thinking was she right to present this momentous news wearing a knitted Fair Isle jumper? Too late now, the eyes of the world were upon her, she composed her face into what she hoped was a serious countenance and began . . .

I have been instructed by the Prime Minister to reveal the outcome of 5 years research into trivia pollution. In the scientific world we have for a long time become concerned by the increased use of meaningless and inane phrases on mobile phones. I will cite only a couple of examples, as they are now too dangerous to use, and will, from midnight tonight become illegal.

'I'm on the bus.'
'I'll be home in 5 minutes.'

A full list of all harmful phrases will be delivered to every household tomorrow. The list is also available on the government website. All phrases on the list are banned. Anyone caught uttering these phrases will receive an automatic prison sentence of not less than six months, such is the grave situation we find ourselves in.

As you may be aware, wool is a natural absorber of sound. Sound is effectively vibrations of the air. The constant use of the phrases mentioned above, all uttered at the same pitch and frequency has caused a constant ripple of air to be created, a bit like a tidal wave. This phenomenon has been named the Gelling Inane Ripple, or GIR. Five years ago when the research started the GIR strength was 12, now it has increased to 32. At any level past 25 the GIR causes wool, in both its natural and manufactured state to disintegrate. You may have noticed your woollen clothes starting to unravel or holes appear, this was not caused by an increase in the moth population, but by the GIR.

However, for sheep the GIR causes their skin to become peppered with holes, from which they eventually die. The GIR therefore, has obvious devastating consequences for the farming community as well as the textile and cosmetic manufacturers.

There is hope however, tests have shown that with careful conservation and recycling measures the GIR effect can be stabilised and eventually reversed. Therefore, alongside the banning of certain phrases the following measures will be put into immediate effect:

1   Dedicated recycling containers will be placed in every city, town and village for all lanolin products to be collected. These include hand creams and lipsticks. Lanolin is the sheep's natural defence against water. Extra layers of lanolin also serve as an effective barrier to the GIR. All sheep will have extra lanolin rubbed into their skins by the members of the special sheep task force.

2   All mobile phone covers must be made from wool: existing jumpers, curtains, carpets etc must be utilised for this purpose.

3   Travel to sheep and wool producing countries is banned for all citizens. This includes Australia, New Zealand, and of course, Belgium.

4   Sheep are now a protected species; they cannot be eaten under any circumstances. Farmers will receive compensation for their losses.

5   Every household will be expected to keep at least one sheep. However, those persons living in flats will be provided with a communal flock.

6   All citizens will be required to attend lexicon training to increase their vocabulary.

7   Insomniacs must count rabbits.

8   Val Doonican, Noel Edmunds and Frank Bough are outlawed.

If you wish to become a member of the sheep task force please visit the website at WWW.BaaBaa.co.uk.

I thank you for your time and attention. I know that together we can bring the GIR under control, but for now I will transfer you back to the newsroom.

Thank you Dr Gelling. Now we continue with the rest of the news:
Taunton police set up roadblocks to stop sheep rustlers.
Mint sauce stock prices plummet worldwide.
Yves St Laurent launches 'Bo-Peep' collection.
Thousand flock to church as panic hits.

Back in the studio, Dr Sandra Gelling disentangles herself from the microphone. Walking outside to the cold night air she heads for the nearest park, and after carefully making sure there is no one to observe her, she surreptitiously removes her mobile phone from her coat pocket. With excited, trembling fingers she rings stored number 1 and whispers lustfully, 'I'll be home in 5 minutes, get out the sheepskin rug.'

DADDY'S LITTLE GIRL
Mary Linney

Jenny pierced her skin with the hypodermic needle and told herself, *this is the end.*

Life had been sheer hell in the last twelve months and she now intended to end it once and for all. Her mind went back to her childhood days...

She was always 'Daddy's little girl', but as she grew up into her teens she met the wrong kind of people and got into the wrong kind of habits frequenting places of low morality which had appalled her parents, especially Daddy who had high hope for his favourite daughter.

Then there was Robert, her boyfriend who had let her down so badly.

She had thought that life with him would be for the better till she announced that she was pregnant.

'Oh no Jenny! I can't take on the responsibility of you and a baby. This has to be goodbye. Forgive me, but that is how I feel. Forgive me please.' And goodbye it was.

Having told her parents about the baby she hoped that they would be able to guide her through her months of pregnancy. Instead, Dad told her to pack her bags and get out saying that there was no room in a decent home for a common slut, adding, 'You are the lowest kind of person anyone could have for a daughter.'

Jenny went slowly upstairs to pack her belongings. Everything stuffed in her case she just went numb with shock.

She sat on her bed and looked around the room for the last time. A place where she had always been happy in as a child.

She'd wandered round the streets for nearly two hours before managing to get this flat.

That was nearly two weeks ago. Now, she'd made her mind up. She had reached the end of her tether.

The hurtful words her father had said to her still rang in her ears. 'Common slut. Common slut'. How could Daddy think that about his little Jenny? Her arm throbbed where she had inserted the needle. She lay on the floor in a semi-conscious state. *It won't be long now before I'm out of my misery.* She felt her arm going numb and her head felt like it was going to explode at any time.

Looking around the squalid flat, her eyesight dimming she could see empty wine bottles strewn all over the floor, dirty tea cups with drops of tea still in them. Some cups had milk soured rims round the inside having been there for over a week. Same with the ashtrays which were filled to capacity.

'Sod it all,' said Jenny in little more than a whisper, 'I've had enough,' she heaved a sigh then sank into a deep coma . . .

Meanwhile, Jenny's mum and dad were discussing the events of the last few weeks. They were getting rather worried because apart from one phone call they had not heard from her. She had seemed very depressed.

'I don't think I can cope on my own!' Jenny had told her mother.

Before she rang off Jenny left her phone number and her new address.

As Mum was getting ready to go to town she suddenly felt the urgency to get in touch with Jenny, fearing that there must be something terribly wrong. Picking up the phone she dialled Jenny's number. Her heart began to pound as she listened to the phone ringing in the flat, sounding in her worried state more like an alarm bell than the buzz of an ordinary phone.

'Come on Jack, get the car out. We must go and see if Jenny is alright.'

Within minutes the car was in the driveway and they were on their way to town without hesitation.

'Maybe we were a little harsh on her Jack,' said Mrs Brown. 'She is our daughter, our own flesh and blood. I feel that we didn't do enough to help her. She seemed so depressed when she phoned home.'

The car came to a halt at the traffic lights.

'Come on, come on, change colour you blighter,' Jack shouted.

He was very irritable and started the car up erratically giving Mrs Brown a nasty jolt.

'Take it easy Jack,' said his wife, 'we aren't going to get there any faster by being irritable.'

'Sorry,' he mumbled under his breath.

It had started to rain. First in spots then all of a sudden the heavens opened up . . . 'Drat it,' said Jack, 'what's going to happen next?'

They arrived at the address that Jenny had given them over the phone.

It was a very large house that had been converted into God knows how many flats.

'This looks a right dump,' said Jack. 'Look at the curtains, they haven't been washed in years. They're ready for falling down. Fancy our Jenny living in a place like this. I can't believe it.' His voice quivered as he felt a large lump in his throat.

'Come on Lass, let's go and see what's happening.'

They got out of the car and climbed the six steps leading to the dismal looking house.

Ringing the door bell they waited for what seemed to be ages. The bell sounded right through the building. It was like a nightmare.

At last it was answered by a tall black haired woman, very untidily dressed.

'Yes, can I help you?' she asked, in a rather unfriendly voice.

'Oh, sorry to bother you, but we are looking for our daughter Jenny. Is she in, we would like to speak to her,' said Jenny's mother.

'I don't seem to have seen her today, but I can check her room for you if you like,' said the woman abruptly.

She had a bunch of keys fastened on a belt round her waist. They seemed to Jenny's parents to make a horrible ringing sound as she mounted the steps to the second floor landing.

This woman looks more like a prison wardress than a landlady, thought Jenny's mum noting the harsh stone like features on her face.

'Jenny's flat is number six, here we are,' said the woman inserting the key in the door. As it opened Jenny's mother felt the blood drain from her body observing the shocking scene in front of her.

'My God! What has happened to my poor Jenny?'

Jack ran straight over to where his daughter was sprawled. He felt for a pulse in her neck.

'She's barely alive,' he shouted. 'Get an ambulance quickly,' he bawled at the landlady.

Within minutes the deafening wail of police and ambulance sirens sounded.

The flat seemed to be full of people and absolutely chaotic.

The ambulance men gently lifted Jenny onto a stretcher and took her downstairs to a waiting ambulance.

They arrived at St Bridge's Hospital in minutes where she was rushed straight into intensive care.

Jack and his wife showed up five minutes later feeling drained, they both went directly to the reception desk and waited.

The tall blonde receptionist was on the phone but seeing the anxiety on the faces of Jenny's parents put it down and went over to them.

'Can I help you in any way?' she asked in a soft spoken voice.

'Yes,' said Mrs Brown wiping the tears from her eyes.

'My daughter Jenny was brought in about ten minutes ago. Can you tell her about her condition?'

'Well my dear, she is in intensive care at the moment. She was really in a bad way. The specialist is with her now. I'm afraid it's going to be sometime before we can tell you anything specific. Why don't you both go and get a cup of hot tea? You look as though you need one. The doctor in charge of her will let you know something eventually when all the tests have been completed.'

After six cups of tea and four hours later the receptionist called out.

'Mr and Mrs Brown, can you come to the reception desk. The doctor would like to see you both.'

Just then a tall slim man in a white smock came towards them and led them to a small office.

'I'm Doctor Charnley, you are Jenny's parents are you? Pleased to meet you although I can't say that I have any good news for you. Your daughter was four months pregnant. I'm afraid she has lost her baby. Jenny was in a serious condition when she was brought in, she is still in a coma. If she does regain consciousness there is always the risk she will be brain damaged. Now, would you like to go and see her. You can rest assured we will do everything in our power to get her well. But don't raise your hopes too high.'

He beckoned to them to follow him, leading them down a long corridor into a well equipped intensive care unit.

'Here is your daughter Mr and Mrs Brown. You may stay with her for a while.' He was silent for a moment, then added, 'Jenny is going to need a lot of care and attention if she does pull through.'

'You can rely on us doctor,' whispered Jenny's mum wishing that they had not turned her away when she needed them most.

They gazed down at the silent pale forlorn figure recognising that it was their daughter. She had a very sweet childish look on her face. Mr and Mrs Brown went over to the bed and kissed Jenny on the forehead;

she looked like a rag doll but her face was peaceful and so still. Sitting by the bed they hoped that by some miracle she would open her eyes.

Jenny's dad suddenly broke down sobbing like a baby, uncontrollable. Dr Charnley was about to make his exit, changed his mind and went over to the heartbroken father.

'Come on Mr Brown, getting so distraught isn't going to help your daughter one little bit. Try not to get upset for Jenny's sake.'

'I'm sorry,' blurted out Mr Brown, 'I can't believe that my Jenny has let us down so badly. She was such a lovely child and we were a very close family.' He added, 'For the last year or so she has been mixing with undesirable characters. We did warn her about drugs and drink but we couldn't get through to her. What are her chances of recovery Doctor?' he sobbed.

'It's hard to say at the moment. We will know better if and when she regains consciousness,' said Doctor Charnley scratching his head.

Just at that moment Jenny stirred, her eyes flickering, her lips moved but no words were audible.

'She's coming round,' gasped Mrs Brown excitedly, tears running down her pale drawn face.

'It's us Jenny, your mum and dad, can you hear me Jenny?' she took hold of Jenny's hand, it felt lifeless.

'She could be like this for days,' said the doctor. 'But let's hope that I am wrong. I will get Nurse to bring you a nice cup of tea.'

'Nurse Templeton,' he called to a young nurse who was passing the open door at that moment. 'Mr and Mrs Brown would like a cup of tea, and oh yes, some biscuits, would you be so kind?'

The young nurse nodded and proceeded towards the ward kitchen.

'Thank you Doctor,' said Mrs Brown, 'you have been more than goodness itself and we appreciate it.'

The sad figure of Jenny's dad was sat by the bedside, his face in his hands sobbing quietly.

'I wish she was the same as she used to be when she was a little girl, loving and affectionate towards us, she was always Daddy's girl.'

Just then Jenny stirred, her eyes opened for a few seconds. Then she spoke in a rather muffled child-like voice that was barely audible.

'Mummy, Mummy, can I have my dolly and teddy to play with.'

Then she slipped back into semi consciousness.

Her mum and dad looked with amazement at Doctor Charnley.

'Does this mean she is going to be alright Doctor?'

'On the contrary,' replied Dr Charnley, 'it means simply you have got your wish. You have got your little girl back. She is and will always be five years old.'

FUTURE IMPERFECT
Neil Campbell Roper

Sanjira looked at herself in the long wall mirror and liked what she saw: tall, slender and feminine, with long black hair, and almond shaped eyes, she knew she was eagerly sought after at the world fashion shows. She felt fortunate indeed to be a model.

After slipping on a red silk negligée and a gown, she wandered casually to the *multimedia* room, where she lazily reclined on a sofa, and on a remote control dial, pushed the button called *fashion*, after which a fashion show was displayed on a large wall opposite her. She was noticeably absent from it. After about ten minutes watching it, Sanjira moved to a special apparatus, that resembled a reclining dental chair where she put on a special helmet, which connected directly to her brain and had to fasten a safety belt round her waist. Suspended from the top of the helmet was a forward mounted visor covering her nose and eyes. In her hand she gripped a remote control responsive to the pressure of her fingers. It was popularly known as *Little Emo* (short for emotion), though its real name was the PBC, or *personal brain computer*. It responded directly to the emotions of the brain, so, as Sanjira desired herself to take part in a fashion show in a London hotel, images of her in a leopard skin, formed in the visor; then she pressed another remote control button, the *smellies*, a device that produced smells corresponding to the pictures, in this case, exotic perfumes. On another remote control dial were buttons for sound, popularly known as the *muso*. At last, feeling that her senses were gratified, at all levels, Sanjira enjoyed the emotions of being applauded at an exclusive fashion extravaganza. After five minutes she felt she had had enough, and imagined herself on a remote island listening to Aboriginal music and the sound of the surf. Letting her fantasy wander to other sensual delights, Sanjira eventually tired and pressed the *stop* button.

Feeling she needed a drink, she walked over to a wall where a control panel, marked *kitchen* was placed. After she'd pressed that button, a whole array of symbols with drinks and dishes appeared. Sanjira pressed *orange juice and scrambled eggs*, then sat down and waited until a robot trolley with metal arms on it, suddenly rolled itself into the room from the kitchen with the items requested. With the year 2080, all necessity to cook manually, and even to activate rubbish disposal had been removed by computer software. Sanjira felt truly relieved, not being a cooking addict.

What she didn't know was that her flat was also filled with concealed cameras and every movement was monitored in a government control centre. Inner city crime rates had soared with overpopulation, thus forcing the government to enact tough new laws of control.

Outside, Sanjira became aware of a vague commotion, so opened the windows, again by remote control, of her kitchen that overlooked the street. Far below she spotted a massive crowd of dishevelled and rowdy people of all ages, chanting what sounded like . . . *want a roof, want a job*. They had come from the Thames end of the street, but simultaneously from the other end, another crowd entered, until she was horrified that they clashed right under her window and started fighting among themselves.

Immediately Sanjira went to the videophone and called the police, who said they would come as soon as possible.

As soon as she put on the TV news, the announcer reported that large gangs of unemployed and homeless were roaming the streets and that citizens should stay indoors until the police could bring them under control. The recent birth of a privileged technocracy coincided with rising prices, which meant that more and more people felt excluded from housing and paid work. Sanjira, because of her extreme beauty and wealthy Eurasian parents, had no worries in any sphere.

Now however, she was supposed to take part in a fashion show in central London. With the angry shouts and fighting of the crowds below, she was unable to move anywhere. On the TV news it showed people being attacked in various suburbs, with police struggling to cope. In parliament, the government decreed that all immigration from countries outside Europe was now at an end, and huge detention centers were to be erected hastily.

Sanjira felt she would like to have a child, but the European government had recently introduced a law that a license was needed for each child and that only one was permitted per married couple. All children by sexual intercourse were forbidden, and huge state laboratories with test tube babies had been built.

Sanjira currently had no partner and anyway disliked test tubes as a method of producing children.

She felt a prisoner in a world of virtual reality, with gangs in control of the streets. She could not even get to work.

A CRUEL TWIST OF FATE
Liam Heaney

Steve Richards drove the powerful red Porsche 911 into the pebbled drive of the large Victorian manor house. He was filled with nervous anticipation. This would be the first time he had seen Kristina for over six months.

The drive curved smoothly round to his right, a line of tall, thin cypress trees verging the drive on each side. These towering evergreens came to an abrupt end as the ivy-covered house came into view. The front lawn was extensive and it had the appearance of being well maintained. Sitting up alertly in the centre of the lawn were two heavy muscular doberman dogs. To his far left he saw a grey headed old man come out of a large greenhouse which was well-stocked with plants. On seeing the old man, the two dogs sprang to their feet and bounded off after him. It seemed strange to Steve that the old man took no notice of the approaching Porsche, as the broad treaded tyres of the solid shiny wheels crunched noisily over the pink pebbled stones of the drive. Perhaps he was a little deaf, mused Steve. The old man disappeared from sight along a narrow paved pathway at the side of the house, with the two dogs obediently following behind him.

As he brought the car to a sudden halt alongside a row of dwarf conifers, Steve noticed a white laced curtain in one of the upstairs rooms slowly move to one side. It was just possible to make out the face of an elderly woman before the curtain once more covered the whole window. Steve had no idea who this woman could have been, as Kristina's mother had been dead for more than a year. It was probably one of the housekeepers, he thought.

As he gingerly climbed out of the car, Steve could hear the dogs barking some distance away. He headed to the front door of the house half expecting to see the dogs rounding the corner of the house to investigate the stranger in their territory. After a short time the barking stopped and he reached the door unhindered. It was a large double door of solid mahogany and it looked as if it had been recently varnished. There was a faint smell of polyurethane varnish in the air which momentarily aggravated Steve's sinuses. He lifted the grand, shiny brass knocker which suitably adorned the door and firmly knocked it twice. As he waited for a reply he casually looked around. He noticed the profusion of purple flowers hanging resplendently on the clematis that clung to the trellis to the right and left of the door. It was a marvellous specimen of a plant which clearly relished its sheltered position close to the house.

He was about to knock again when the door suddenly opened and a gaunt elderly woman gazed sternly at him from the darkness of a seemingly spacious hallway.

'Yes, young man, what do you want?' she brusquely exclaimed.

Steve was somewhat taken aback by the sharp tone of this cadaverous old lady, but he did not show it in his reply.

'Could I see Kristina please?' he said with clear composure.

The reply he received was uncompromising and to the point.

'There's no one here called Kristina. You obviously have the wrong house, my dear man!' and with that she hastily closed the door.

Steve stood quietly for a few moments looking out across the lawn. He was perplexed. He certainly had not anticipated such a cold reception. Of course, he had not told Kristina that he was coming. His visit was intended to be a surprise and so was the car. But why had the old woman denied that Kristina lived here? No, he couldn't have made a mistake. He had been to this house on a number of occasions and although there were evident landscaping changes to the garden this was undoubtedly Kristina's house.

Suddenly, he remembered the dogs. He slowly looked round, half expecting them to be at his heels but they were gone. He moved further out into the drive and carefully scanned the lawn and the surrounding shrubbery. The dogs were nowhere to be seen. Steve was now becoming very concerned. From his arrival at Boulevard Heights things just didn't seem to be fitting together. What was going on?

In an attempt to clarify in his own mind the situation in which he now found himself, Steve furtively made his way to the greenhouse. Perhaps the old man he had seen earlier had returned and he would be able to give more assistance about the whereabouts of Kristina than had the old lady.

A flood of happy memories came to Steve as he walked the short distance to the greenhouse. He recalled the time that he had met Kristina about eighteen months ago at an environmental conference in France. He had enjoyed her company as they sat over a candlelight dinner in a cosy little French restaurant shortly after the conference had ended. Their relationship in those few short days together had blossomed and he seemed confident that they would continue to see each other for sometime to come. Although, he had not seen Kristina for the last six months he had written to her on several occasions expressing his desire to see her again when he returned from safari in Africa.

In Africa, Steve had been looking at the behaviour patterns of big cats, particularly the cheetah. The nature of his work made it almost impossible to phone her regularly. Besides, the scientific study of the fastest animal on land was quite clearly a full time occupation. In actual fact it had occupied his attention for many long, arduous months. Kristina had written to him over the months telling him about her environmental projects and about her short trips to European cities in connection with her work. She had certainly not mentioned anything about the old man or the old lady who now appeared to occupy her house. This was her house as it had been left to her by rich and successful professional parents. Her father had built up an extensive shipping business and her mother was an eminent lawyer. From his conversations with Kristina, Steve had gleaned that her parents had always worked closely together. Both had tragically died together in a horrific car crash some six months before he had met Kristina.

Steve had now reached the open door of the greenhouse. From the entrance he could see a vast array of flowers in clay pots of various sizes. The pots stretched some way back and the colours of the flowers and the prolific green foliage gave the greenhouse a jungle-like quality, steamy and humid. As Steve moved further into the greenhouse, he perceived a considerable increase of temperature and he was somewhat overpowered by the sweet, heady aroma of hundreds of flowers. In fact, the heat and intoxicating scent quickly enveloped him and he felt distinctly unsteady on his feet. The scene before him started to spin uncontrollably and he reached out to gain support from a wooden shelf that held a range of prickly cactus plants. But before he could make his way back to the open door, he collapsed onto the gravel floor of the greenhouse.

When Steve regained consciousness he found himself in a darkened room, lying on his side, his hands tied behind his back. As he slowly rolled over to sit up straight, he was keenly aware of a strong, damp earthy smell which aggravated a dull headache. He could hear faint noises which sounded like rats scurrying about the floor. He also sensed the presence of something or someone in the room with him, although he couldn't see anything at this stage.

He couldn't understand why his hands and feet were tied. He could only assume that someone was making sure that he could not escape. With brute strength he freed his feet. He could feel an intense stinging sensation in his ankles. He had peeled some of his skin away in his desperate effort to get free. Slowly he pushed himself up using the cold dank wall of the room to give him leverage. Some distance from where he was standing he could see a wafer-thin line of light which indicated the bottom of a door. With his back still to the wall he used his hands to feel his way carefully along the length of the room. This would eventually bring him to the door, he thought. He had made only a few unsteady movements along the wall, when he abruptly fell over something solid lying in his path. His whole body experienced a shuddering, agonising spasm of pain.

For some moments, he lay prostrate on the rough cobbled floor, unable to move. When his pain eventually eased, he turned slowly in an attempt to identify the object which had caused him to fall so heavily. As he moved closer to it, he could feel a gentle glow of body heat. Moving closer still, he could hear faint breathing. He was lying beside someone! An alarming thought flashed across his mind. No, it couldn't be! He moved closer to the body, seeking to ease his mounting concern. He deliberately knocked against the body, which elicited a short, feeble groan. Steve instinctively discerned that this was the groan of a man and not a woman. Although, still perplexed and agitated he was greatly relieved. It was not Kristina.

As the person beside him slowly became conscious, Steve desperately wanted to find out who his captured partner was and what he was doing in this damp, starkly unpleasant place. As these thoughts came to him, the person on the floor groaned again and exclaimed, 'Oh, my head aches. Where am I?'

Steve replied quickly attempting to give some reassurance.

'Are you okay?'

Steve's eyes were somewhat accustomed to the dark at this stage and as he spoke he could see the man beside him gradually sitting up, holding his head in both hands and massaging it gently.

'I feel as if I've been hit with a baseball bat,' came the reply.

'Where on earth am I?' he asked again as if for the first time.

'I'm not sure,' said Steve. 'I think we've been put in here for safe keeping.'

Steve noticed that the man beside him had a short grey beard.

'That wouldn't surprise me,' said the man still rubbing his head. 'I'm Frank Burns,' and he reached over slowly in the darkness searching for Steve's hand.

'My hands are tied,' said Steve. 'The name's Richards, Steve Richards.'

'Let's get your hands free,' said Burns, as he moved with great effort, reaching for Steve's wrists.

As he attempted to release the tight bindings, which seemed to be some sort of thick gardening twine, he began to tell his story of how he got there.

'You know, we've had this place under surveillance for well over a year now. It's a beautiful house with magnificent gardens but unfortunately it very much looks as if it has been commandeered by a drugs syndicate. I called at the house today to speak with the owner. I was immediately shown to a room and that's all I can remember.'

'But there's only an old woman in the house,' suggested Steve, hardly believing what he had heard.

'Obviously, she's a cover and so is the old man you may have seen working in the greenhouse,' he added as he continued to grapple with the strong twine. There was more to Frank Burns than Steve first realised.

'Do you know of Kristina Evans?' Steve quickly asked.

'You know Miss Evans?' Burns quizzed.

'It was Kristina I came to see. I met her a number of months ago and I've been in touch ever since.'

Was Burns a detective or an agent?

Burns appeared to ignore the question posed, as if he was stalling for time to think of an appropriate answer. Finally, he freed Steve's hands.

'We'd better get out of here pretty quickly,' he added, 'the people we're dealing with are ruthless and will stop at nothing.'

This was easier said than done. The door, under which Steve had initially seen the thin stream of light, was solid and evidently bolted from the outside. As both of them explored the room they soon realised that this was a boiler house of sorts. There were pipes lining the walls. The pipes themselves weren't large enough for a person to squeeze through even if they had been able to disconnect one from another. But the fact that they were there suggested that they lead to another room or to the air outside. This gave them greater encouragement to find a way out.

After much frantic searching, Burns found a small ventilation grill, which lay hidden behind a pile of rotten wooden planks. Pushing through a thick, meshed clump of brambles they were eventually able to crawl out into the open air. It was bright and sunny outside and both men were momentarily stunned by the intense light, having emerged from almost complete darkness. They were breathing heavily from their exertions. However, the air outside was at once invigorating and the strong aroma of freshly cut grass, mixed with the intoxicating scent of blossoming flowers gave them a real sense of freedom.

They stood against the outside wall of the building for some monuments adapting to their new surroundings. In the distance, Steve could see rows of glass houses bordered by tall, mature conifer trees. Burns sensed Steve's keen interest in the scene before him.

'That's where they grow the cannabis,' he volunteered.

This guy, whoever he was, seemed to know a lot about what was going on and in one way, it was reassuring for Steve to be with him.

Burns continued, 'This house and its grounds are ideal for such an operation. It is remote and isolated. It is hidden away in the countryside. The grounds are expansive and those greenhouses can't be seen from the front of the house. If you did see them you would never suspect what they were being used for.'

Steve found it difficult to take all this in at one go. Escaping was now a priority. He had read about drug barons and the care they took to ensure that their clandestine dealings were kept a secret. He needed to get away from here. But he still wondered how Kristina fitted into the picture. Was she also part of this elaborate drugs enterprise? He found that hard to believe.

As if reading his thoughts, Burns added, 'That girl Kristina you mentioned earlier owns this place, as I'm sure you know. Some say she's behind the whole operation.'

'You're not serious?' Steve was stunned. 'Are you sure?'

Burns did not reply. He had noticed someone emerging from one of the greenhouses in the distance. He grabbed Steve by the arm, urging him to move forward.

'We'd better move quickly or we'll be seen. Let's go! We'll head for those trees. They should give us some cover.'

Steve ran off first, quickly followed by Burns. As they made for a safe hiding place among the group of trees, Steve noticed the thick treaded tyres of a car which had been positioned behind one of the other outbuildings some distance from the house. It had been carefully covered with camouflage netting. In any event, someone had neglected to secure the netting properly and the wind had revealed a single wheel of the object beneath. Steve recognised it as his car. Realising their apparent good luck, Steve suggested that they make their getaway by Porsche.

'You must be joking! You own a Porsche?' exclaimed Burns in disbelief.

'Well, actually yes! I have a friendly bank manager!'

They agreed that this was their only means of getting away quickly and safely. They scanned the grounds for guards. There were none. In minutes they had removed the camouflage netting and were inside the unlocked car. Steve removed a spare key hidden discreetly beneath the driver's seat and pushed it into the ignition. The powerful engine of the machine roared as he hastily put it into gear and pulled off disturbing the pebbled stones. As he rounded the corner of the house into the drive, he observed in his rear view mirror three athletically built men dressed in denims, brandishing stubby, semi-automatic weapons. They were pursuing the car with arms outstretched ready to fire and two doberman dogs were running alongside them.

Steve pressed hard on the accelerator. The car sped off at high speed, one bullet ricocheting off the large rear spoiler.

'That was a close shave!' exclaimed Burns with an evident sense of relief.

'Too close for comfort, if you ask me,' replied Steve as he skilfully manoeuvred the car into the narrow country lane.

'Let's get out of here,' insisted Burns.

As the car sped along the winding lane both men in their own particular way felt confident that the whole affair at the manor house would soon be resolved. Kristina would be vindicated.

Suddenly, their thoughts were abruptly interrupted. From the bushes, close to a large gnarled oak tree, came a devastating hail of piercing bullets, emanating from two powerful weapons. Their force and number shattered the windscreen of the Porsche, as it slowed to negotiate a sharp bend in the country lane. The driver lost control and the car swerved off the road, breaking through the thick hawthorn hedge, eventually coming to an abrupt halt in a field of ripened maize.

From behind the oak tree two hooded gunmen emerged. They cautiously approached the badly damaged car, their AK-47's held in readiness. But having seen that the ambush had been successfully executed with military precision they lowered their weapons.

'Let's head back to the house, we'll clean the scene later when we report back,' the taller of the two men said gruffly.

'We've shut those two up permanently,' his accomplice added with malicious delight. 'Kris will be pleased!'

QUADROPHENIA 2: THE ROAD TO NOWHERE
John Lee

The weekend had just rolled round again and the following week I had booked off as holiday and was planning to go to Amsterdam. It was Webby's birthday and the Jolly Boys outing was all set to descend on the M20 nightclub.

Half past eight and the coach arrived, we all jumped on with beers being passed around. I shouted for the driver to turn the radio up and off we set. Webby already looked worse for wear, courtesy of the BMW that we'd all chipped in for him. I was glad I didn't have to drink it because Baileys, Malibu and whisky all in one glass sounded like a right stomach cruncher.

On arrival at the nightclub our main concern was getting Webby into the club. The drink had hit him and he could hardly stand up. After nattering to the bouncers and convincing them that Webby was fit enough to enter the club, we made it inside where we were greeted by a giant statue of a pirate, which we had to queue around.

What a night, vodka and Red Bull was being drunk like it was going out of fashion as we danced the night away. Later on, it came to my attention that I hadn't seen Webby since gaining entry into the club. After searching the club I found him propped up in the toilets being supported by his brother.

Taking this as a sign to leave I gathered up the rest of the lads and then hit the burger van before boarding the coach and leaving the nightclub. After finally dropping everyone off I climbed into my pit, where as soon as my head hit the pillow I was asleep.

The following day I realised that in my drunken stupor that I had lost my passport, which I had taken with me to gain entry into the nightclub. Frantically I phoned round the lads and the coach company in an attempt to find it.

In the meantime I was sitting watching the news, where to my horror I watched two planes crash into the twin towers in New York. Watching these tragic events unfold was disturbing enough and the implications it had on my following week meant cancelling my plans of heading to Amsterdam.

It was then that I decided to hit Camber Sands, passportless and meet my mate Brad who along with his room-mate Mike, was armed with the magic stash. After being in their vicinity for only ten minutes I found myself in hashish heaven and was dancing round the caravan to the time warp. You didn't smoke this green. It smoked you, and was so potent you could smell the vibes back in Jamaica.

The next few days were spent watching planes crashing into the twin towers, during this period Brad and I maintained a stoned up trance of a silence not uttering a word in respect.

I was living in a hell hole of a caravan where I couldn't even take a dump because there was no bog roll, the floor was scattered with fag ends and I was forced to use my cream puffa jacket as a pillow, which smelt like a brewery, courtesy of our drunk and stoned up antics.

By now I was longing to return to work and the relief was immense when my mate Mitch and his girlfriend Laura came to pick me up and headed home for the sanctuary of a real bed.

It was then that I returned to work as normal, feeling quite stressed out after what should have been a week's holiday. After returning to work I also resumed a lifestyle of hitting bars on a Thursday night and clubbing on a Friday and Saturday night. I was burning myself out.

During this time Jimmy White was scheduled to be playing in Herne Bay in exhibition at £10 a ticket. I snapped 3 tickets up and headed down there with my brother and best mate Eddie.

After witnessing a couple of lack lustre frames, the three of us headed to the bar. It bought back memories of when I used to attend the club for the school discos. Eddie cracked a joke that we were in luck that evening as there was a seven of diamonds playing card stuck to the roof of the ceiling, which was quite remarkable seeing as the ceiling was about 60 foot high from the floor. Drinks were ordered in copious amounts before returning to see Jimmy knock in 13 reds and 13 blacks. I was amazed at the sheer genius of the man, and that break made it well worth the entrance money.

After departing the King's Head, we headed for Somersets where by this time the beer was well and truly flowing. It was there that I was introduced to Angel who had caught my eye. For some reason I thought there was something different about this girl yet because I was shy I didn't go for it.

Still the evening was made all the worthwhile by watching Jimmy so I tried to forget about her.

Returning to work on Monday I proceeded to open the post and parcels as per normal whilst listening to the radio. It was then that I began to hear voices and thought I was being talked about on the radio.

Freaking out I telephoned my boss convinced I was having a nervous breakdown, who in turn decided to give me the rest of the week of work with stress.

At this point I made an appointment to see my GP and asked for a blood test because my boss asked if there was a possibility that my drink had been spiked which might have explained the way that I was feeling.

The results of my blood test came back all clear, which was a relief, despite this I still felt stressed. Frustrated that I was unable to get any more time off work I decided to empty my desk and walk out, I had no contract of employment and I could take no more.

The following week my luck seemed to have taken a turn for the good. I went on a double date with Eddie's brother for a meal with Angel and her friend Hazel. I was loved up and convinced that she was the one. Yet I was too shy to open up and tell her how I felt. I just couldn't tell how she felt about me, but I knew one thing, I was infatuated with her.

After the meal the date progressed into the four of us going clubbing, it was there that Angel began to flirt with another bloke. Incensed by this I left the club and headed home via a taxi all by my lonesome.

Days later Webby and I decided to go up to a football match and watch my beloved Tottenham Hotspur play. The game was a drab affair with the end result finishing 0-0. The main event that stood out for me during the game was at half-time when I looked up at a director's box and saw who I led to believe was Angel and Hazel. This sent my brain spiralling off in a different direction which I just couldn't understand as I was under the impression that Angel was uninterested in me and I just couldn't fathom the pair of them out.

Directly after the game Webby and I headed for the train station, we made it to London Victoria and once we had boarded the train was forced to stand, as there were no seats. It wasn't long before a fight kicked off with the opposing fans trying to take on Webby and I. Outnumbered we were forced to jump off the train at the next incoming station. It was then we faced a new dilemma with the railway police confronting us. I then kicked off demanding that they got the Prime Minister down at the station because I was burning with rage at the fact we had paid for our tickets and were forced to stand and the fact that we were the innocent party and the victims. I was demanding that they sent another train to pick us up.

This did not get us anywhere, well in fact it did but it was handcuffed and shoved into the back of the police car where we were carted off to the cells for the night.

What a week, I had walked out on my job, I lost the girl and to top it all I had been nicked. Talk about the road to nowhere.

THE SECOND THUNDER
David Russell

Tom silently watched the feverish evening sky from the cracked window by the fireplace. The cloud's unrest moved the treetops along the road from west to east, then back again. The odd, uneven glimpse of stars passed through the airborne mist and complimented the waning moonlight on the car.

Unusually quiet, the only sound came from the next room, the rhythmic beat of a train slowing down. *Brief Encounter* was the film. The atmospheric ambience of its black and white was reflected in the window he watched. His own lined face looked back and told him something he already knew.

Thunder tore through the tender night air. Tom pulled the fading curtain over the glass as the rain began to fall. He stood quiet for a moment, looking around him and took a slow breath in, as if saying goodbye. Lifting the glass on the side table and placing it to his lips without thinking, he saw it was empty. It didn't matter; he liked holding it. The reflection of the rain on the window streaked beautifully down the side of the armchair as he touched it with the tips of his fingers, feeling the comfort of the old leather. Sitting down, glaring blankly into the glass, he put it up to his eyes and looked through it at the space where the curtain edge had caught, revealing the corner of the window. Faint moonlight and running water spectacularly glowed through its contours, shining like a fall of diamonds from a long forgotten dream.

The telephone rang. Sharply darting his eyes in its direction below the faulty table lamp, he paused for a moment, thinking. Gently lifting the received to his ear, he swallowed.

'Hello?' There was no response for a brief few seconds.

'Hello, Mr Millard?'

Exhaling sharply, he replied, 'No.'

'Sorry love, must have the wrong number.' The dial tone swiftly replaced the almost familiar female voice. Holding the receiver by his side, he listened to the fading buzz.

Throwing it down onto the telephone again, Tom stepped into the living room where the television flashed its singular shades amid the black of the walls. He took the glass he still had in his hand and clumsily poured a second drink, hearing the melodramatic tones forcing themselves upon him. 'There's still time . . .' There was no time at all.

Switching off the set he returned to the other room while swigging back the bitter whiskey. The rain had momentarily ceased. Grimacing from the alcohol, he sat awkwardly on the old chair and lifted the book that lay half-read on the floor. He opened it and read aloud the words that jabbed at his eyes. As each word passed with increasing difficulty, he suddenly stopped as he reached the final, penetrating lines . . . 'and to prove out almost-instinct almost true: what will survive of us is love'.

Following the simple words over and over, he treated each one as a stranger, unknown to the darkest realms of his sight. Perhaps he didn't see them at all. In either case, he left the book open upon the table below the freshly-vacant glass. Pacing again to the window, drawing back the curtain, he looked to the silence, searching. Whispering, almost to himself, he said, 'If you can see the moon, at least we both do.'

He gently shut his eyes from the glare of his reflection. Almost at once the piercing ring from the telephone sounded once more.

Pausing for a second time, he quoted the final line of 'An Arundel Tomb' as he could not have before. As he slowly picked up the receiver, the heart inside him ringing more fervently and persistently than the irritating phone, 'What will survive of us is love.'

He breathed once, heavily, but needed to say nothing aside. The sweet, yet somehow shrill voice on the other end spoke two words only, but they too, were enough.

'I'm sorry.'

Swallowing hard, a strange kind of knowing, perhaps, Tom put the receiver beside the phone before walking into the hall and opening the front door. The unwelcome chill of the night was unmistakable, but out there was a certain calm. He had always loved the night.

Stepping out to stand in the wet of the already fallen rain, he turned to the transient clouds, and his eyes did not blink.

He looked, and looked, and kept looking until he knew the sky, until he knew the movements of the clouds and the stars that played hide-and-seek.

Thunder roared for a second time. The night remained quiet.

A Candid Story
Susan Booth

She thundered down the street, her brats in tow. Together with enormous biker boots, evil tattoos, a greasy mass of rats tails and several piercings, she envisaged the build of a Russian shot-putter or worse still a Japanese Sumo in fancy dress. The streets were totally deserted apart from silent graffiti and tipped over dustbins spilling out all manner of disgusting aromas. All the kids on the estate had scarpered as the foul mouthing trio approached, apart from the odd rat scurrying through rubbish oblivious to the terror that reigned.

The atmosphere reminded me of the film *High Noon*. I'd watched it several times as a teenager.

One small boy was a little slow getting away, and with one swift grab, he was hoisted up by his shirt collar. The swollen, grubby fingers adorned with several knuckle-duster type rings held him like a worn out rag doll as he dangled lifelessly, a look of sheer terror plain for all to see as he held his breath while the three of them gripped him by the throat and wrists.

'Give me ya money,' she bellowed at the gaunt little face.

'I ain't got none missus, honest.'

'Ya lyin',' she squawked as he was dropped to the ground with a thud which sounded like a sandbag being thrown onto gravel stones from a great height. The boy remained silent as one of the brats gave him a swift kick in the back. 'Ya get me some money tomorrow, 'cause if ya dunna I'll pop ya eyeballs right out of ya face and squeeze ya scrawny little neck till it cracks, do ya get me?'

'Yes missus,' the boy choked pitifully, doing his best to hold in tiny petrified sobs.

The trio continued their journey, homing in on the next victim with greedy evil eyes slit like in the characteristic of vultures circling their prey.

I was there in my capacity as a reporter working for the Daily Newcomer on inner city street crimes. As I turned to the boy someone was already helping him to his feet. 'We should get him to hospital,' I said. The agony etched on his face was evident as the boy held his ribs, his skinny hands scuffed and bleeding. The older male scooped him up into his arms. 'I'll take care of him now missus, he's me brother.' It felt weird being called missus. I was barely thirty-years-old myself and it made me feel about ninety, but I was concerned for the boy.

'Really he needs medical treatment. I can take you, my car's just around the corner.'

'Coppers'll ask questions missus, just leave us be.'

'But shouldn't you tell the police about this, your brother's been seriously assaulted?' I said anxiously.

'Make matters worse, please just go.'

I couldn't leave them, and as I scanned the road towards the edge of the estate, the tormentors were turning the corner for a repeat performance. For a moment we all froze to the spot, then somehow I gained my senses, 'Come on run,' I screamed. We fled for our lives.

As we approached my car it was apparent a brick or some object had been hurled through the rear windscreen. Luckily the automatic unlocking system still worked and my wheels were still intact. 'Get in the front quickly.' The rear seat was a mass of broken glass. How on earth I managed to locate the ignition I'll never know, my hands were shaking violently.

Just as I was about to accelerate the perpetrators caught up, one clung to my door handle, the other leapt on to the bonnet. I accelerated anyway and after several hundred yards travelling at considerable speed they were eventually flung off. I watched them through my rear view mirror roll away, almost landing side by side into the ditch. No one dare breathe or speak until we were safely out of danger. I stopped the car and finally drew breath.

For the first time I saw the older male look at me with complete relief and gratitude. As I studied him closely for the first time it struck me how incredibly breathtaking his appearance actually was. His skin colour was the deepest bronze, smooth almost velvet like in texture, he had the most amazing, piercing blue eyes, like deep sparkling sapphires in contrast to his skin tone and shining black hair closely cropped around his handsome features. My guess was that he was in his late twenties as I tried to avert my gaze away from those penetrating pools of blue staring intently at me now.

'We're going to hospital, I'm not taking no for an answer again, surely you can't want your brother to suffer like this?' He nodded, knowing there was no choice. A few hours later as the nurses cared for the younger boy we stepped into the hospital grounds and sat together both staring into each other's eyes. As he reached forward to touch my face . . . the director shouted, 'Alright, cut! Well done guys, we'll finish filming tomorrow.'

ANDERSON JOE - NOVEMBER 1940
F Lyndon

Although heavily pregnant with her third child, Fanny Sumner still looked a small wiry woman as she stood anxiously at the entrance to the Anderson shelter, where her two daughters, Betty, aged five and Beryl, aged three, slept. It had been a long night of heavy bombing. Fan had had little or no sleep in her makeshift bed, the drone of the German bombers as they went overhead, the sounds of explosions in the distance, but most of all the worry that her husband, Joe, was out there working his night-shift at the BSA. Birmingham had taken a battering and now Joe was late returning from his shift.

Fan peered at two figures in the distance; as they got nearer she could see they were ARP wardens. She started walking towards them, calling, 'Where have the bombs fallen; anywhere near the BSA? My Joe's not home yet.'

The wardens looked at each other, 'It's been a bad night,' one called. 'A lot of areas have been bombed. Your husband could well be helping out, BSA Golden Hillock Road is one of the places in trouble.'

Fan's stomach turned sick, she had such a bad feeling that something terrible had happened. There was no way she could wait, she had to go and see for herself. She stopped only long enough to go into the house where her mother, too crippled with arthritis to get into the air raid shelter, had spent the night, wrapped in blankets, in the cupboard under the stairs. Fan grabbed a woollen scarf and a thick coat that belonged to Joe. 'Mom, see to the kids when they wake, give them some breakfast and make sure they have a wash. I'm going to see if I can find out any news of Joe, I think the BSA's been hit.'

Burdened by her unborn child, Fan walked the distance as quickly as possible. So engrossed with her own worry, barely noticing the amount of damage to houses and buildings as she passed, firemen still playing their hoses on smouldering remains, and the ashen-faced women standing bewildered, hanging onto the belongings they have managed to salvage. Good-hearted neighbours ushered them and their children into their own undamaged homes, as always the first thing offered would be a cup of tea and the warmth of the fire.

As Fan approached Golden Hillock Road her worries and fears increased. A great part of the BSA factory was heaps of rubble. There were many fire engines, ambulances and hoards of people scrabbling amongst the rubble. Teams of men formed lines to remove bricks where their workmates, friends and neighbours were buried; there was a smell of burning and death in the air. She ran forward as a stretcher passed, hands held her back as she tried to get close enough to see the face of the man. For several hours she stood waiting for news. Although bitterly cold Fan was too numb with fear to be aware. Many hours later she allowed herself to be taken home, although totally exhausted by now, she could not be persuaded to go to bed, instead she sat in an armchair by the fire listening and waiting for someone to knock on the door and tell her Joe had been found. Wherever he was, hospital or shelter she must be ready to go to him. So for the next three days she trudged to the edge of the factory, watching and waiting as bodies were brought out, checking the names of survivors and dead as they were identified.

Fan awoke on the fourth day; she had fallen into an exhausted sleep, the first night's sleep since the air raid. Once again she knew, after her morning's routine of giving her two girls breakfast, washing and dressing them, she should leave them in the care of their granny and set off to the BSA. Deep in her heart she knew her husband was dead. Rescuers knew there were still many people not yet recovered and no hope of them being alive. Her brother, Ted, had been to see her two days ago, he worked alongside Joe in the same department, and he and Joe always walked to work together taking the shortest route along the canal. He told her that the air raid siren had sounded when they were about halfway. Knowing the BSA was a prime target, Ted suggested they skip the night's work, go for a pint, then return home. Joe was in favour but then decided against it. 'I hadn't better, Ted, we need all the money I can earn at the moment, we still need a pram for the babbie.' So they parted company, Joe carried on to work and Ted returned home to his family.

Even as Fan trudged wearily to wait and hope for news, she was aware of backache and niggly pains. After three or four hours waiting alongside other women who each hoped for news of missing husbands, sons and brothers, she knew she was in labour and needed to return home. At times on the way back she stopped to rest, for the pains were becoming strong. There were several tasks she had to do before she took to her bed to await the birth. Her daughters, Betty and Beryl, would have to be fed and tucked up for safety in the Anderson shelter, for the air raids seemed to be happening nightly now without fail. She prepared her bedroom ready for the midwife to be called, washed herself and changed into clean clothes. The two children were amusing themselves, knowing it would soon be time to go to the shelter. Fan took the children out of the back door into the small garden and down the steps into the shelter, by now used to the procedure they huddled down into their bunk beds, under the heavy coats they used as blankets, and would soon be asleep.

Fan returned to the house to help her mother prepare her chair under the stairs, in case the air raid got too close for comfort. Her intention was then to go to the house two streets away to warn the midwife she would no doubt need her services that night. Too late, the wailing of the siren started. She prayed it would only be brief. It seemed no time since the warning siren before she heard the first bomb explode. It was loud, it was close; she grabbed an old coat and ran outside into the garden. One more blast put the fear of God into her, roof slates crashed around her head; she gave one leap straight into the shelter and landed in a heap on the floor at the bottom of the steps. Fan lay stunned, desperate and in great pain, as the raid continued. The engines of the German bombers and the noise of the bombs hid her cries for help as, alone, she started to give birth. It seemed hours before the cries of Betty alerted the neighbours that Mommy was hurt and please would someone help.

The midwife arrived to find Fanny lying in a pool of blood on top of her old coat, still fully clothed. As she part undressed her, she could see the baby was almost delivered, only the mother's underwear had held and supported the half-born child. It was a boy; tiny, pale and so weak his cry was more like the mew of a kitten. As the midwife wrapped the child in an old towel, she said, 'Afraid he's not here to stay.' Kind neighbours helped to get Fan to bed, her baby close by, only expected to live hours at the most she needed him next to her. Early next morning the baby was baptised, named Joseph after his father. Despite all predictions and to the amazement of many, Joseph did not die. Although still very small he continued to thrive and became known throughout the neighbourhood as 'Anderson Joe'.

As Joe trudged along, arms outstretched, head hung low, for the second time that day pushing his old pram loaded with coke up Kingston Hill, he thought to himself, *some way this is to spend my birthday*. Still just a slight figure at seven-years-old he had to carry out tasks that many a lad twice his age would find difficult. He looked a sorry sight, little thin legs with scabby knees, grey socks wrinkled down to his ankles. His feet were dry thanks to his 'Daily Mail' boots, but did they hurt! Two sizes too big so they would last, but so hard; where they rubbed were blisters as big as a shilling piece. Joe tried not to think of them, hoping he wouldn't notice the stinging pain too much. He took a breather to wipe his runny nose on the sleeve of his jacket, he also glanced back fearfully, he was sure he had spotted Old Man Benson the school truant officer, when he was back at the coke yard. This was a favourite place for him to hang about, it was easy to spot the children who should have been at school but had been kept at home to fetch coke or coal. Poor Joe seemed to spend more time away from school than at it. He didn't really like school, mainly because he had lost so much time, he wasn't able to read or write very well, so he was always in trouble or laughed at. At least in school he was dry and reasonably warm. He set off again after his rest. Getting the pram moving was hard for one of the front wheels had started to wobble a lot. The wind whipped past his ears as he pushed hard, it wouldn't have been so bad if it was blowing from behind, but it was against him.

He glanced round again. 'Oh no, I'm sure that's Old Man Benson, please don't let it be, don't let him catch me again. He said my mother will be in serious trouble if I'm kept off school to fetch coke. It's not my fault I have to do all these jobs but I don't want her to be in trouble, what would we all do if she was sent to prison?'

Mom spent so much time at Mrs Bassett's house where she cooked and cleaned for their family. Without the food and extra money she earned this way they would all have been much worse off. Betty and Beryl looked after him, kept the house clean and washed the clothes. As for Joe he never seemed free of all the chores expected of him, such as fetching errands and coke, not only for his mother and Mrs Bassett but any neighbours who were willing to pay a few pennies. It all added up to help his widowed mother to cope. The wheel of the pram seemed to be wobbling more, he jammed the pram against the lamp post and bent down to have a look. Joe tapped the centre of the wheel with his 'Daily Mail' boot, hoping it would stay on until he got home. It was so cold, he pulled at the old socks he wore on his hands as gloves and pushed them up his sleeves. Giving his runny nose another good wipe on the sleeve of his jacket he went back to the handle of the pram. His heart started to beat like crazy, it was Old Man Benson, unmistakable in his long Mac, trilby hat and carrying a briefcase, he was watching him not too far behind. Please let me go home, don't let him catch me, Joe prayed. He dug his toes in, pushing as hard as he could, and as he started to run in his panic, the wheel wobbled more and more. Down the kerb he pushed, running across the road, but as he bumped up the kerb on the other side the wheel came off, the pram tilted and part of his load of coke spread across the pavement. Joe was in total panic now, how was he going to get home? He would be in such trouble if he left the coke but if he stayed to pick it up, Old Man Benson would get him. Joe's little body strained as he took up the weight of the pram on his back as he bent to put the wheel back on. As he started to pick up the scattered coke he sobbed. Old Man Benson didn't say a word, he stood about ten feet away, just watching. The rest of the journey home was a nightmare, he could not go very fast, and had to keep kicking the wheel back into place every few yards. His hated enemy continued to follow him all the way home without saying a word, and Joe wet his pants with fear. When he reached his front door he wedged the pram so it wouldn't roll, ran into the house - thank God his mother was there. He ran straight upstairs and hid under the bed, trembling and crying, he tried to listen to the voices downstairs, terrified his mother would be taken away.

The next day he went to school, just as his mother had promised he would, his face scrubbed, his hair plastered down, clean jumper and short trousers, although any movement that opened the tear in the seat of his pants showed quite clearly he didn't have any underwear. After the horror of yesterday, Joe was pleased to be going to school, especially as he had managed to grab an apple as he passed the fruit shop; he would eat that in the playground at lunchtime.

So Joe's life continued, he always had to work hard to earn cash any way he could to help his family, as he got older and matured he wasn't so afraid of everyone. He didn't have too much spare time, but when he did, he had plenty of friends, always one of the lads up to mischief and having a laugh. Joe very often mixed with the older lads, one of these, Jackie Powell, was his hero. Jackie was at work, so of course was better off, he had various ways of earning money and had managed to buy a battered Austin 7 car. At the age of 11 Joe had his first go at driving along with his other friends, Johnny Hewet and Kenny Folding. On spare ground, off Garrison Lane, they all crowded into the car and took turns at being taught to drive by Jackie Powell. It was hilarious, the ground was strewn with rubbish, bumps and holes, and they were all thrown about in the back as the driver tackled obstacles with more and more courage. This went on for some weeks, whenever Jackie had managed to *borrow* some petrol. Sadly all this fun came to an end, dustbins had been placed to form a racecourse, each driver trying to better the time achieved around the course by the previous one. Kenny got too ambitious, lost control and smashed into a concrete post. The poor Austin 7 was past repair, never to be driven again but left as a plaything for the very young boys.

Jackie wasn't happy unless he had some type of vehicle to drive. Eventually he ended up with an ex-army lorry complete with gun turret carriers on the back. Jackie was always ready to share his good times with the other local lads and arranged to take eight of them, including Joe now aged 13, away to the seaside for the weekend. The trip down in the back of the lorry, then a visit to the funfair, was a huge success until they all decided to have a go on a very large helter-skelter. Everyone except Jackie went down the slide the correct way, on a coconut mat. Jackie lost his at the top, it slid away before he could sit on it and he arrived at the bottom shouting and hollering with pain. He hopped around holding and rubbing his backside. When the lads discovered he had no seat in his pants and friction burns on his bum, they gave him no sympathy and laughed until they cried. As the pain of Jackie's burns eased a little and they wanted to continue the day's outing, it was evident they needed to cover Jackie's exposed backside. Joe ran to a stall in the fairground and persuaded the chap there to let him have a large sheet of brown paper and a length of rough string. Back with his mates they set about tying the sheet of paper around Jackie's waist, no one dared to laugh outright but there was a lot of tittering behind hands. They all bought fish and chips and took them to eat, sitting on the beach. Of course a good bit of time was spent watching any young females passing, when they would whistle and call remarks, enticing them to come and sit with them on the sand. All went well until Jackie had to stand up to walk to the toilet. A crowed of girls started to laugh. His face was blood red, he stormed off, shouting they were all to go back to the car park.

The good humour of the day had gone. As all eight tried to settle down to sleep in the back of the lorry, and Jackie's backside still very sore got trod on, bickering broke out, developed into loud arguing and finally fighting. It wasn't long before someone called the police, a constable arrived on his bike and ordered them off the car park. In time everyone got over the fallings-out, and the day was talked and laughed about for years to come. Eventually Jackie started to mature and the young kids weren't invited to join him on his trips, especially after he sold his lorry and bought a Jaguar Mk 9. No more driving lessons for anyone.

Despite these good times, Joe always remembered he was the man of the house and it was up to him to take care of his mother and sisters. At 14 onwards Saturday night out was something to look forward to. Tonight was special, he had his new trousers to wear. For some months he had been working in his spare time for a local butcher, delivering meat, sweeping the floor, scrubbing the block, no task asked of him was too much. Still small for his age, to ride the delivery bike with a basket on the front to hold the meat, he nearly always stood up to pedal; he could ride faster this way and get back to the shop for his next errand. The butcher appreciated his hard work, knew Joe was dependable and paid him five shillings a week. With two half-crowns clutched in his hand he used to race home. One half-crown he gave straight to his mother. The other one was his to save, for clothes, kept in a jam jar under his bed. Each Friday he tipped his savings out, counted and re-counted, working out how much more he needed to buy his chosen item. Slowly he was acquiring more clothes, he always looked after them, folded or hung neatly when not being worn. To polish his shoes was a labour of love, and more time was now taken with his hairstyle, Brylcream was a must!

So here he was ready for his Saturday night out, that morning he had been to Fosters on Coventry Road to buy the trousers he had been saving for. He had had a good scrub and soak in the tin bath in the kitchen, now he stood admiring his reflection in the misty mirror in his mother's bedroom. Smart shirt and tie, new trousers, shiny shoes with hair to match, he was ready to hit the town. Joe had discovered, sometime ago, that girls weren't the nuisances he had thought. He enjoyed the banter and the chat-up lines he was developing, but hadn't as yet had his first girlfriend. Tonight he was off to see a film with his friend, Geoff Smith. Geoff had always been a bit better off than Joe and most of the lads of their age group. His grandmother, Mrs Boffey, kept a greengrocery shop and because she allowed the local cinema to advertise with a poster the film being shown outside her shop she was given two free tickets, which she gave to Geoff. That's where they were off to tonight. They would have a bottle of Nut Brown beer each hidden in their pockets to sup as they watched the film, and the thought of three penn'orth of chips each on the way home.

Life was getting easier now, sisters Betty and Beryl were both in steady jobs, bringing home a wage each week, at last Joe was 15 and ready to leave school, this was his last day. For once he was in luck, already he had a full time job to start on Monday. This was where his sisters worked - Hughes Biscuit Factory. At last Monday arrived, Joe was up early, spick and span ready for his first day. He had finished his tea and toast and was waiting for Betty and Beryl to finish theirs. As they set off together he glanced back, his mother was watching from the front doorstep, she gave a smile and a wave, and Joe felt six feet tall. Unfortunately this feeling of tallness didn't last very long. When he arrived at the factory he was taken along with the group of new starters to be shown his duties and issued with a pair of overalls, so big, the body part almost reached his ankles, the trouser legs had to be turned up so much they hardly existed. After the girls had packed the biscuits into boxes it was Joe's job to stack them onto a trolley. Ten boxes high, fifty boxes to a trolley, this could only be achieved by Joe standing on a wooden box to reach the top layer. Then of course the trolley had to be pushed to the storeroom. The older women who worked there found the picture of this bright, quick, happy little fellow in huge overalls, peering round the side of the boxes of biscuits because he couldn't see over the top, such an amusing sight he quickly became a favourite. For the first time he was the spoilt one; he was given treats and extra tips for pocket money, he thoroughly enjoyed himself.

Joe got on well with all the girls, but especially he took a shine to Irene. At first they smiled at each other as they passed. Soon Joe was looking for her at break time; eventually they started to chat each day. Joe plucked up courage to ask Irene to go to the pictures, he was surprised and chuffed when she agreed. The Brylcream and shoe polish was in full bloom. For twelve months Joe felt sure he was in love and Irene continued to be his girlfriend. Still being very young at this time, the call of his single mates began to make him restless. It was eventually Joe joining a skittle group that ended the relationship. This was also the start of Joe's Teddy Boy era. Drainpipe trousers, velvet collared jacket, shoelace tie, thick crepe-soled shoes and bright coloured socks. Again the Brylcream was in evidence as it helped to hold his DA hairstyle. He sauntered along the monkey run with his mates, impressing the girls with their stylish gear. Saturday night was rock 'n' roll night, the only place to be was out dancing. Here Joe's quick feet made sure he was never short of a dance partner. After he had rock 'n' rolled the evening away, his chosen girl was escorted home for a quick snog in the entry. He was enjoying life too much at the moment to think of going steady.

After a couple of years Teddy Boy fashion diminished for Joe, he now felt his stylish ways were more suited to being a Mod. With much enthusiasm he dedicated himself to being the smartest Mod going. Crewneck sweater, cut-away collar shirt and winkle-picker shoes completed the Italian-look suit. At last the Brylcream took a back place on the shelf. It was the best day in Joe's life when he bought, at last, his longed for Lambretta scooter. Astride this, as Joe rode down Garrison Lane he knew just what it felt like to be a millionaire.

It was these years that Joe was thinking about and had been for the past hours, as he sat huddled, tired and cold during the night at Good Hope Hospital, awaiting the birth of his first child. Josie, his wife, this girl he had met in his Mod heydays was in the labour ward and had been, for what seemed an endless time. He thought of the first time he had laid eyes on her at Laura Dixon's Dance Studio, he quickly fell in love. They had enjoyed six years together going through the courting game, engagement, and finally marriage. He was worried for Josie now, he wanted the baby to arrive and to know everything was OK. At last the waiting room door opened and his name called. His legs actually shook as he walked with the nurse to enter the ward. Josie lay in bed, she was pale and tired-looking but her eyes shone with pride as Joe was introduced to his baby son. Martin James Sumner, weighing in at 8lb, born 4th November 1969.

Later after the great excitement following the birth of Martin, Josie his wife rested and Joe studied every tiny feature of his baby son. Again he counted fingers and toes. Gently he traced with his own fingers, his tiny ears, shape of his head, the softness of skin and silky hair. A great love for this tiny person surged through his body, leaving him so full of happiness and pride. Slowly Joe began to feel almost sad and subdued, he thought of his own father, that he had been denied the joy that he himself now felt with the birth of his son. He compared his own birth and realised the depth of a father's love, a love that he had never known. Joe vowed there and then that he would devote the rest of his life to providing for his wife and son, determined they would want for nothing. In this very emotional state Joe felt a peace and warmth settle, he had a great feeling of comfort and closeness, he knew for certain his father was there, sharing the happiness at the birth of his grandson.

TRUE BILL
Mary Cathleen Brown

Thomas Fleming took his cigar out of his mouth savouring the sweet smell. He did not speak. The other man, his lawyer, who had brought him the unwelcome news, began to make the best of it.

'Of course, it's an annoyance, but . . .'

'Well yes, it's an annoyance,' said Fleming dryly.

Fleming leaned over and knocked off the ashes from his sweet-smelling cigar. He was silent as his lawyer continued.

'What has Hammond got to support his opinion that you pinched $3,000 from the Hammond estate?' His memory of something somebody said 12 years ago and an old check.

'Hammond's a fool. I'll punch a hole in his evidence in five minutes. What we want is to get the case up at the head of the calendar as soon as we can. Get it over! Then, if you want revenge, we can turn around and hit back with *malicious prosecution!* I suppose it will be in the evening papers.'

'I suppose it will, since the findings of the Grand Jury were reported at 11 this morning, plenty of time for the first editions. Then I'll take the early train home. My wife,' he paused.

'Doesn't Mrs Fleming know?'

'No, I didn't want her to worry over it, so I didn't say anything. Of course now she must know.'

'I know how you feel about Mrs Fleming, but rather than have her disturbed, I'd compromise on it. I'd pay him, I'd . . .'

The lawyer raised his eyebrow. 'This time I think Hammond is honest. I guess he really believes he has a case and you'd be encouraging blackmail to compromise. Now, don't let Mrs Fleming take it to heart. Tell her I say it will be a triumph.'

Tom replied, ' Amy keeps me in order. She insists that I shall be her best. It appears that my own best isn't good enough for her.' This she would indignantly deny, and indeed justly, for Thomas Fleming stood on his own legs morally in his community. In the 10 years of their married life, no doubt her ideals in small matters had created his. With his indolent good nature, he had found it easier to agree with her delicate austerities of thought than to dispute them.

So it was no wonder that going home on the train he winced at the thought of telling her that Hammond had prosecuted him criminally for misappropriation of funds as trustee of old Mrs Hammond's estate. The trusts had been closed at her death and the estate handed over to her son, the same Hammond who *thought he remembered* hearing old Smith say, 12 years before that he had paid the Hammond estate $17,400 for a parcel of land, whereas Fleming's trustee account put the sum received at $14,400.

Tom gritted his teeth as he sat there in the train planning how he should tell her. Her incredulous anger he foresaw and her anxiety, the anxiety of a woman. He damned Hammond in his heart and pulled out his evening paper. There it was, in all its shamelessness of the blaring headline. *A Leading Citizen Indicted!* and so on. The big, black letters were like a blow in the face and Fleming felt that every commuter on the train was looking over the top of his newspaper at him.

His skin was prickly over his whole body, his ears were hot, every sound amplified. He sank his head down between his shoulders and pulled his hat over his eyes, in pretense of a nap, then suddenly, sat bolt upright. The fact was, he had no experience in disgrace and did not know how to conduct himself.

When the door banged open at his station he swung off onto the platform and plodded slowly up the lane in the darkness to his house. It seemed to him as though his very feet hung back. As the gate closed behind him, he was surprised to see Amy waiting on the porch for him.

'It's blackmail,' Amy said trembling visibly, thrusting the evening news in his face.

'Of course, we shall have no difficulty throwing them down,' Fleming said.

'I don't understand,' Amy said.

It had always been a joke between them that Amy did not know anything about business, so she tried to smile when she asked him to explain.

'Oh,' he said, 'it's simple enough. Smith owed me $3,000, a personal matter. I once sold him some stock, he gave me his note. You wouldn't understand. When he bought this property for $14,400 he made out the check for $17,400. Understand?'

'Perfectly,' she said, 'what a rascal Hammond is!'

'Bates says I'll get out of it all right.'

'Oh, say I am a fool,' she pleaded, 'I would like to think I was a fool.'

'Now let me explain it to you,' Tom said kindly, 'and then you won't be frightened; why, you'll be so sure of me, you'll send out invitations for a dinner party!'

Then, very explicitly, he laid before her the grounds of his confidence. Hammond was a cheap fellow, a short of smart Alec, you know. Briefly, there is no question that $17,400 had been paid to him. Hammond cannot disprove the defense that only $14,400 of it was to go to the trust and the remainder was payment of Smith's debt to him.

'It's all right,' he said, 'it's perfectly safe, as far as the verdict goes; 'but,' he stopped and frowned. It was evident that her demeanor didn't please him. For once Amy did not consult his pleasure. She had her own views.

Suddenly it seemed to this poor woman, her whole slender body tingling with fatigue, as if something fell, shuddering down in her breast. Strangely enough, this physical recognition informed her soul. She heard herself speak, as one falling into the unconsciousness of an anesthetic, hears, with vague astonishment, words faltering, unbidden from the lips.

No, no, came the body's frightened denial.

Then in silence, her soul: *He did it. He did it!*

Her husband put his arm around her to comfort her, but she drew away. 'No, stay away from me! Please don't! Please. Just go away!' She was inconsolable.

Thomas Fleming, dumbfounded, couldn't find his wits for a reply before she had slipped away from him and heard the door of their bedroom close. He stood at the foot of the stairs for a moment and then went back into the library to smoke.

Amy's eyes opened painfully to the dark. She seemed to be sleeping soundly when he awoke the next morning and began creeping about, not even daring to kiss her lest she might be disturbed. She waited until she heard the front door close as he hurried to make the dash for the eight-fifteen.

Poor soul! She had no thoughts but that one. She had some coffee, dressed and went down to the library, recoiling involuntarily at the sight of the corner where the accounting ledger was kept on the shelf.

The flexible, red-covered book drew her hand with the fascination that comes with remembered pain. She shivered as she opened the book. It occurred to her, with vague surprise, that this book would probably have settled the whole matter if Tom had only remembered it. Here were the entries about the Hammond trust.

Borrowed $3,000 from the Hammond Estate to pay back money borrowed from Ropes Estate.

No doubt restitution must be made, but restitution would not change the fact of what he was and what he had done. She dropped into his chair and thought, *I never knew him.* She wondered if she loved him, not that it mattered whether she loved him or not.

So the day passed and this is where Tom Fleming found his wife when he returned home.

'Amy,' he began, but she checked him.

'Please, I must speak first. Please don't interrupt me! I shall pay the money back somehow. Of course I shall not betray you. My paying it shall not be a telling of the truth because unless the truth comes from you it cannot help you. It must be your truth, not mine.' She stopped, trembling from the effort of so many calm words.

Thomas Fleming looked doggedly at the floor. He bit his tongue, tasting the blood. 'I'll suppose you'll want a separation?'

'Get a separation, why we are separated. We can't be any more separated that we are.'

'You'll stay with me then. I thought you despised me.'

'No, I don't think I despise you.'

'You really mean you won't leave me?'

'No, I won't leave you!'

'Of course you no longer love me,' he said roughly.

She turned sharply from him.

At that he broke, poor soul, which would have denied itself for very shame. Love brought him to his knees, arms around her waist, his head against her breast, his tears on her hand. 'Amy! I will pay it back. Oh Amy, Amy.'

YOUNG LOUIS HAS A SMALL HANGOVER
IN HIS SMALL WORLD
Robert Creamer

Young Louis has a small hangover. He sits on the park bench on the embankment staring out at the slow river, his eyes fixed in a pained squint, body motionless in a paralysed slump. A small boy of around six or seven is running about scaring fat pigeons into attempted flight and periodically making loud squeals of delight. John, sitting next to Louis, eyes the child with disdain and shifts his large frame on the bench.

'It's not an unpleasant sound,' says John, a prospective cheeriness in his voice.

'What isn't?'

'Child hitting concrete. I'm hoping soon that kid will fall flat on his face.'

'Why don't you push him over John?'

John turns his face towards Louis. 'You just want to see a big, fat guy running after a little kid, pigeons scattering everywhere.'

'Well, now that you've brought it to mind, it does have a certain visual appeal. Harold Lloyd could have made a comeback with that one. No, I just don't like kids and that scream is just cutting right through me. I'm tired, I got virtually no sleep last night and I need peaceful sounds, not screaming children. I just don't understand the popularity of children amongst adults at all. Since they stopped sending them up chimneys I don't see their usefulness in modern society. And I didn't like kids that much when I was a kid either.'

The child moves away from them both for a moment. Louis leans back on the bench, pushes his curly fair hair behind his ears and listens to the rustling of the trees.

'I don't know,' says John, 'I quite like kids normally, it's just that particular one.'

'Because you were popular as a kid.'

'Yeah, I was, well they thought I was funny. The fat funny kid. But the appeal of that wears off after a while. As an adult too. Like when I was a panel beater.'

'I thought you enjoyed that?'

'I did, but they wanted flat and I only did concave or convex. So I quit and decided to go to college. Now I frequently argue against all the class about books that I haven't read. I'm very convincing. College, it's all about arguing with conviction, very little to do with knowing the right answer.'

It's a mild December day, Christmas is a few days away, John and Louis and Jerry have been wasting time, walking through the town looking in windows, side-stepping children and otherwise generally taking the lackadaisical approach to life.

'You should quit your building society job Louis and come to Deaford college with me and Jerry. It's great, Jerry starts a new course about every couple of weeks. He'll never finish one, so conceivably he could be there forever. I think he hopes he'll get a girl that way.'

'Will he?'

'No. Well, he might do if he made the effort. Maybe. No. Probably not.'

'I can't believe we lost him. Where could he get to so fast?'

'Exactly. Probably gone home as fast as his little legs would take him. But this is what he's like at college. He's there, and then he's not there. Just disappears, a vanishing act. I can't figure him out sometimes, because he's very popular, they all like him, they think he's cute, apart from Sara. She just thought he was creepy. He liked her though, maybe that had something to do with it.'

'I think when you like someone, you automatically become creepy to them, it's a sort of divine mockery at work. But Jerry's good at bull**** when there's nothing to gain from it. I like that.'

'Yeah, but you do that all the time too.'

'So we're all losers.'

'I don't think we're all losers,' says John.

'You're far too optimistic about the world though.'

'Yes, but I think you and Jerry are far too pessimistic about the world.'

Louis resisted a slight sneer. 'Jerry the short, spotty, overweight, asthmatic smoker that eats too much fried food and chocolate? Known to inhabit sofas for lengthy periods and found in regions where TV is plentiful? Lives with his folks with their pink council house door in Puddlestown, unknown centre of the universe? That Jerry? I wouldn't say he was too pessimistic about the world.'

'Maybe not, but he can be very witty.'

'Yes, I agree, you and I find him bright and funny, girls find him creepy.'

'No, that was just that one girl . . . and maybe her friend. And that was only because he liked her. Anyway, what's your excuse?'

'I get depressed that Jerry's a lonely guy due to die of a heart attack. And apart from that people find me very irritating after prolonged exposure.'

'That's simply because you tell them what they don't want to hear all the time.'

Louis shrugs. 'Honesty, it's a curse.'

'That's not honesty, it's just tactlessness.'

'Same thing.'

'So do you want to drift back towards town?' asks John.

Louis looks towards the direction of the town. He thinks of his job, monotonous and seemingly eternal. Having no illusions about the joy of other occupations, he assumes he will stay where is he, believing he will never be able to break out of the pattern. He watches the six-year-old whiz past them again. 'Not really,' he replies, 'let's wait and see if that kid falls over. Besides, I'm weak from the effects of drink and a hollow life.'

'I didn't think you drank that much?'

'I didn't. I'd never make it as a lush, I'm too easily afflicted.'

'So have you had the whole week off?'

'Uh-huh.'

'Do anything?'

'Not really. Apart from last night. Although I suppose that wasn't really doing anything either.'

'Yeah, but sometimes that's quite good, just doing nothing.'

This last comment of John's draws another look of disdain from Louis that does not go unnoticed.

'Well I think it is,' says John. 'But perhaps that's where you differ from Jerry, because at least he always has that small burst of enthusiasm for something before he decides that it's futile after all, whereas you think everything is futile right from the start.'

'It comes from being a lapsed Catholic. You still believe in the crucifixion but you no longer believe in the resurrection. It gives you a dim view of humanity.'

'That argument doesn't seem to make sense, one without the other.'

'Of course it makes sense. It's easy enough to believe that someone was crucified because lots of people were crucified and apart from being cruel and in keeping with human nature, it's a physically tangible thing that everyone knows is possible. It's something quite ordinary in a way, whereas the resurrection is a miracle, ie something miraculous, supernatural, a remarkable occurrence, not ordinary.'

'But I always thought you were still quite religious.'

'I am still quite religious, I believe in the crucifixion. I'm halfway there.'

'But that's like believe in evil without believing in good,' protests John.

Louis waits for him to make his point.

'Well you can't have one thing without the other,' argues John.

'Why not?'

John pauses before answering. 'Well . . . I suppose it's like a degree of measurement really. There are acts that are considered evil and then there are other acts that are considered less evil and so on until you have good.'

'Aha,' says Louis, 'so good is just less evil is it?'

'No, that's not what I said, what I mean is . . .'

John stops mid-sentence, interrupted by close footsteps and heavy breathing behind him. He arches his body around on the park bench to find Jerry there, sweating profusely.

'God Jerry, I thought you were some prowler!'

'A prowler?'

'Yeah.'

'In the daytime?'

'Yeah, a day prowler. You can get day prowlers, they work nights and the daytime is the only chance they get to prowl. Christ, you're really out of breath. Where have you been?'

Jerry wheezes on and gestures inconclusively towards the town. This seems to satisfy John.

'We thought you'd buggered off and gone home. So anyway Jerry, do you believe in good and evil?'

'What? What are you talking about?'

'Good and evil, we're into a big, meaningful discussion here so . . .'

'It isn't that meaningful,' interrupts Peter.

'Well, I think it is, so anyway Jerry do you? Believe in good and evil?'

Jerry's breathing has slowed. His eyes move from left to right in thought. 'I believe there's good in everyone,' he finally says.

Peter leans back and takes a good look at Jerry. 'You don't believe that Jerry?'

'Yes I do, well almost, perhaps not you. Almost everyone.'

'No c'mon.'

'What do you mean c'mon, it's Christmas, you have to believe there's good in people.'

'See. See,' says John to Peter.

'Ah, so you don't believe it, you just want to believe it?'

John ignores this question and turns to Jerry again. 'But do you believe in the Devil?'

'Yes.'

'Really?'

'Of course.'

'With the horns?'

'Yes, with the horns and the pointy tail and the cloven hooves.'

'Maybe glasses?' offers Peter.

'Only if he's reading.'

'The Devil hasn't got time to read, he's got a full-time job making people miserable.'

'Yes,' says John, 'and tripping you up.'

'Ah no, now you're getting mixed up, that's not the Devil, that's God. God is the one that's forever sticking his foot out. The Devil's more your carrot and stick deal. Temptations of flesh, power, money, eventually followed by the eternal flames of Hell.'

'Hmmm,' ponders John, as the little pigeon-chasing kid zooms past again, 'the eternal flames of Hell eh?'

'Think of the fossil fuels they must get through,' says Jerry, finding room on the bench to sit down.

John and Louis exchange a glance.

'Can we change the subject?' asks John.

'Why? It's a cold, winter's day, all this talk of Hell is keeping me warm.'

Despite Louis' protestations they nevertheless fall into silence. The sun comes out from behind a cloud and shines down briefly on the world. Each of them has their own thoughts, quite different from each other and quite different from the people walking past. John is the most positive, he thinks he must always be positive. It's the way to be, to be geared up and ready, to take on that English class at college, to be confident, to beat that lecturer at his own game. He knows he can win, get the girl, be successful, make something out of life. He doesn't have many days of doubt. But on days like this he's worried that he'll be brought down by the other two, that he'll stop having fun. It isn't so much Jerry, when Jerry's deflated he just ups and leaves in the middle of what he's doing, he quits and goes back to the council house, he keeps it all within himself. But Louis, he doesn't keep it to himself. Sometimes he's just silent and emanating depression, but at other times he lingers around and with the slightest inadvertent prompt starts babbling on about the misery of the world. He makes jokes along the way, maybe in an attempt to keep it light-hearted, but in John's eyes it doesn't always work.

Jerry has a bad feeling inside, he wants to leave now and he's not sure why he came back and found them. It was OK last night, but now the world is sober and the sun seems bright and yet cold. He doesn't mind Louis and John, sometimes they make him laugh, but it isn't enough. He wants something else, but he doesn't know what it is. He didn't think being nineteen would be like this, he didn't think college would be like this, he doesn't know how to fix it.

Louis doesn't much like working in the building society, he feels so out of place. With John and Jerry it's much better, to see them every once in a while is like medication of some sort, a release where he can almost relax. Even his slight hangover seems beneficial to him, that slight pain above the eyes compounded by the cold of the day, this makes him know he's alive after all. He often thinks of suicide and yet always finds an excuse to not carry it forward. It's just a slight inclination though, he has no real reason to kill himself, beyond any other human being down by the embankment that day. It isn't really the job that makes him think of suicide anyway, he just has morose thoughts, he always has had. Even as a small child, when his belief in God was absolute, he had morose thoughts.

Jerry gets up and stretches, he was feeling cold on the bench.

John looks him up and down and grins, 'You look like shit Jerry.'

'Thanks.'

'Where you going?'

'Nowhere.'

'Well, in the wider picture obviously,' says Louis, 'but I think John meant right now.'

Jerry seems slightly put out. 'I'm going nowhere right now, I just got up to stretch my legs.'

'You only sat down two seconds ago Hyperactive Boy,' says John.

'Oh for God's sake, why are you both hassling me?'

'We're your friends,' says Louis.

John turns to Louis. 'You're the most insincere man I know.'

'No, I was being sincere. I just have the most insincere voice. It's a different thing.'

'How is it a different thing?' asks Jerry, shuffling around on his feet.

'Be-cause,' says Louis sighing and then rolling his eyes and stretching his words out, 'with one you're *being* insincere . . . and with the other you just *sound* insincere.'

John laughs. 'But you are the most sarcastic man I know.'

'Was that sarcasm? I don't think it was.'

'I think it was,' says John. 'Jerry, can you stop moving around, you're making me car sick.'

'You're not in a car,' says Jerry.

'I'm on a bench.'

'That's not a car.'

'It's sort of . . . it has car-like qualities, it has a seat.'

'It's not very mobile.'

'It's as mobile as some of the cars I've had. And you're obstructing my vision of the road.'

Jerry steps to one side. At this moment the pigeon-chasing kid comes darting out from behind a tree on some mission of ornithological destruction and crashes head-first into Jerry's stomach. Jerry gasps as he's winded and just manages to retain some modicum of dignity by not collapsing to the ground. The kid bounces off him and lands on the concrete where he promptly bursts into tears and then gets up quickly and runs off. Louis and John sit down with arms folded and faces contorted, barely compressing their laughter.

'Ah,' says Louis finally, smiling and squinting against the pain in his eyes at the same time, 'the slapstick world in all its glory.'

'God or the Devil?' asks John.

'God.'

'Must have a sense of humour then.'

'Yes, but it's only funny to us because we're not in the middle of it, Jerry's not laughing.'

'God!' gasps Jerry, sitting back down on the bench and holding his stomach, 'that kid's head must be made out of lead or something.'

'Lead?' queries John calmly as Jerry suffers. 'I thought lead was quite soft. Maybe it was steel or iron?'

'Brass,' offers Louis.

'Aluminium.'

'Titanium.'

'Fibreglass,' muses John. 'A fibreglass head. That would really be something.'

'Yeah,' says Louis, 'great for whizzing around chasing pigeons.'

'It's really light isn't it?'

'I think so, yes.'

'Total crap in a crash though, his whole head would have collapsed on impact.'

'Yeah, but Jerry's stomach is quite soft I would imagine.'

'God!' gasps Jerry again. 'Shut up you b*******.'

They fall quiet again. Louis looks up. The sun has returned to its place behind the clouds. *Well, there are some moments to be had in a life he supposes. And if the sun can hide can't he do the same thing?*

John nudges Jerry, now seated again. 'You see those three girls, I think I know one of them from college, let's go and say hello.'

'That's not three girls, that's two girls,' says Louis, 'and they're right over the other side of the river. By the time you get there they'll be gone.'

'Not those girls, those three girls, there.' John gestures towards three girls quite nearby. 'I meant the three girls on this side of the river that are actually *three* girls and not those three girls on the other side of the river that are actually *two* girls.'

Jerry shakes his head. 'They saw you pointing then John.'

'They did,' confirms Louis.

'So? Why is that necessarily a bad thing?'

'It just always is a bad thing,' mutters Louis, arms folded.

'Why?'

'It just is.'

They all see that the girls John was talking about are in fact, looking across at them now, squinting in the light. John grins a big, amiable grin and holds his hand up in a half wave.

'You see, I waved, it's not necessarily a bad thing.'

'They didn't wave back.'

'One did.'

'No, she didn't John, she started to raise her arm and then put it down again quickly when she realised she didn't know who the hell we were. Now we're all condemned as freaks and I'd say they'll be walking away in the next thirty seconds.'

'I bet they don't.'

'Yes they will.'

They wait.

'They're walking away,' says Jerry.

'That's not necessarily a bad thing,' says John.

They laugh together and watch the sun crawl out from behind another cloud for another brief appearance. Louis thinks the sun isn't sure whether it wants to shine. He sympathises with that sense of indecision. Louis isn't sure he ever wants to move again from that bench, he isn't sure he wants to lose his mild hangover. He likes the fact that the ache above his eyes stops him thinking too clearly. He hears a couple of ducks squawking, but no squealing kids. Is the world necessarily a bad place? Not by necessity, but perhaps by habit.

The three of them sit there, on that bench, watching the world drift by, trying to resist the trappings of hope.

Motorway Mike
Diana Stannus

Michael Mason, known unaffectionately to the police as Motorway Mike, parked his van in a lay-by and consulted his notes. His informant, an insolvent double glazing salesman, had reported that the owners of the property went out every Friday afternoon and returned punctually at six o'clock. Ivor the Info said he had only seen the hall and the sitting room during his brief, unsolicited visit, but had noticed some silver, several fine miniatures and antique furniture. Mike had no interest in furniture; silver, porcelain and pictures were his speciality and his expert knowledge was the envy of dealers, both legal and nefarious. He read on: *Mrs Grinley obviously enjoyed a chat. One car, the nearest neighbour half a mile up the lane, no alarm system and no dog.* Good. Access? Mike studied the sketch the helpful salesman had drawn and decided that the flat sunroom roof looked promising and drove on.

Mike parked behind the house and surveyed his surroundings. Lucky, luck, Mr and Mrs Grinley. Surrounded by fields the property was everyone's dream of a country retreat. Senses alert he slowly circled the house, ears strained for sounds other than the breeze stirring the leaves and the birdsong. When he reached the sunroom he ran his fingers over the window frames and found that the Grinley's had been careless. Sweet, smiling fortune. In with no sweat. Out with the screwdriver and gently . . . gently. Got it! He was halfway through the window when his scalp prickled. What was that? Not an actual sound, but a vibration felt, rather than heard. Imagination, he decided after a few seconds of intense concentration.

As Mike slid over the sill, his left knee taking the majority of his weight, landed on the knob of the latch. Excruciating pain shot through him and, as he twisted to relieve the pressure, trapped his ankle under the half-open window, leaving him suspended head down and back stretched agonisingly in space. *Come on, man - move - or you'll be driving with a broken ankle.* As he gritted his teeth and struggled to raise himself, his face was suddenly attacked from above by a wet tongue. His body jerked involuntarily, his ankle slipped free and he slithered to the floor where his feebly waving hands encountered a muscled bulk of thick fur. *God! The brute was huge! I'll murder Ivor the Info for this . . . no dog, he said.*

He tried to sit up but a massive paw held him immobile. 'OK, I surrender . . . call Mr Plod - but get off me!' Mike groaned. All he could see were two brown eyes and open jaws displaying a ferocious set of teeth. *Perhaps I'm dreaming,* he thought frantically, as hot saliva dropped on his face. *If I keep still perhaps he will go away.* A sharp yelp roused him and peering backwards he saw with relief that the dog's tail was wagging enthusiastically. Mike removed the paw from his chest and sat up slowly to inspect his unwelcome companion. The German Shepherd was clearly delighted to see him and Mike noted the glossy coat with the deep approval he gave anything of beauty. But as he stretched out his hand the dog sprang away and whined urgently at the door.

'Want to go out? Hang on . . . let me get at that bolt.' Clutching his bruised knee Mike opened the door and limped after the dog into the back garden where, after bestowing a generous libation on the rear wheel of the van, he ran round in circles barking loudly. 'Oh good grief . . . shut up, you idiot animal . . . trust me to find a dog on his summer holidays!' As Mike sat on the garden bench to recover, the dog trotted over to him and, pushing his broad head into the burglar's chest, gave a deep sigh. 'What's the matter? Locked inside on a fine summer day with no one to play with and you're only a youngster . . . about two I'd say . . . rotten shame . . . poor old chap!' He fondled the dog's ears and smiled down at him, then suddenly remembering the purpose of his visit, took a handful of his ruff and encouraged the dog towards the house. 'Now . . . are you going to tear out my throat if I touch the family silver? Wonder what your name is? Rajah? Rambo? Fred?' There was no response other than the waving tail.

As Mike moved through the kitchen he saw a sheet of paper pinned to the cupboard door. 'Diet?' he read aloud. 'Breakfast: biscuits and gravy. Supper: one pound of meat and . . .' His eyes slid down the page. *And I don't know what I would have done if you and Daddy hadn't agreed to take Tarquin on for a few weeks. Why Paul had to choose the biggest dog in the RSPCA kennels, I'll never know. I'm at my wits' end and . . . .*

'So that's it, Tarquin!'

At the sound of his name the young dog leapt up and put his front paws on the burglar's shoulders. 'Go easy, you great softy, I'm still fragile,' laughed Mike trying to escape the ecstatic tongue.

In the sitting room Mike pulled a large carrier bag from his pocket and looked around with satisfaction. Six miniatures disappeared but, with a sniff, he left two on the wall. Tarquin climbed on the sofa and watched with interest. 'Come on you, get off the *Homes and Gardens,*' muttered Mike absently as several other items of silver and a carriage clock went into the bag. 'Now for the Grinley boudoir.' But as he turned his heart sank when he saw Tarquin sitting on the stairs barring his way. Their eyes were level. There was nothing for it but to move forward naturally, trusting their rapport would hold. Mike placed his foot on the first step and Tarquin solemnly offered his paw.

In the Grinley bedroom an untidy nest had been made on the duvet. 'So that's what I heard,' said Mike bending to pat the dog. 'I screwed up your siesta. Some guard dog. You'll be popular, you bad lad.' There was nothing of interest in the bedrooms so Mike nipped downstairs with Tarquin at his heels.

Leaving the rear doors of his van open Mike returned to the house to collect his bulging bag and the porcelain. Then he realised that Tarquin was missing. He called and whistled, but there was no response. He balked at leaving the dog to roam the garden and adjoining fields, where he heard sheep bleating. As he placed the loot in the van he saw a prick-eared silhouette in the passenger seat. 'No Tarquin, no! I'm not taking you with me . . . come on out . . . back to the house.' Motionless the German Shepherd stared through the windscreen. Mike opened the van door and seized Tarquin's ruff, tugging the dog towards him. The heavy animal leaned to the right to keep his balance and dug his claws into the seat. Mike glanced at his watch. Five o'clock! He should have been on the motorway to Birmingham half an hour ago. He heaved at the dog again, who turned to look at him, his eyes filled with almost human appeal. Mike paused, breathing heavily, 'I can't take you with me . . . I can't have my life complicated by a dog . . . exercise . . . regular meals, there's a lot of night work involved with my job - can't take you where I go - often I'm away for days at a time and I don't use a duvet. Anyway, you'd hate my place. It's in the middle of town with only a backyard and no trees. Next door have got a Pit Bull terrier - a bitch at that . . . and before long you'll be the size of a bloody buffalo! And what's more - you don't belong to me.' As the absurdity of his last words dawned on him, he fell silent. Tarquin's response was a low, contented rumble as he curled up on the seat with his tail over his nose.

The burglar tried to consider his situation calmly. He thought he might be able to lift the dog from the van, but his soul shrank from slamming the kitchen door on those beseeching eyes. But what was the alternative?

He ran back to the kitchen, ripped the letter from the cupboard door and ransacked the larder. Spreading Tarquin's blanket on the floor he piled onto it tins of dog food, a bag of biscuits, the water bowl and a rubber bone. He knew what he was about to do defied all reason, but a voice deep inside was saying - *get on with it* and when he saw a pad and pencil on the dresser, decided to break a golden rule.

A soft grunt greeted his breathless arrival in the driving seat. 'You're lucky, you've no way of counting the cost - and I don't know what I've let myself in for . . but let's get the hell out of here!' With a roar the van disappeared through the gate.

When the Grinley's arrived home from their bridge game they found an open gate, an empty house and a neatly printed note on the kitchen table: *I have taken Tarquin with me at his insistence. As we see it, we have relieved you and your daughter of an unwanted encumbrance. In return for the favour and to pay for the years ahead, I have also removed silver, a carriage clock, selected porcelain and six miniatures. You may be interested to know that the two I have rejected are indifferent copies of originals by George Engleheart (1785) See Sotherby's Catalogue December 1999.*

It took the single-minded, dedicated burglar many hours to reach Birmingham as Tarquin kept removing his left hand from the wheel with gentle, insistent jaws. When Mike finally got the message he was forced to drive one-handed, the other resting on the ruff of the young dog, who had trustingly fallen asleep with his head on Mike's knee. It made gear changing very difficult and there was no question of reaching the handbrake.

Faraway Cottage
Ray Wilson

'Well Lyn, I booked it on the internet, a week's holiday at Faraway Cottage. No electric, no running water, Elsan toilet. Sounds great for a relaxed, no-stress week. It's at North Dambridge, only a couple of hours drive and we are off next Saturday.'

Saturday arrives, right we have loaded the car, Faraway Cottage here we come, sounds great.

We leave the motorway and drive down country lanes. North Dambridge, there's the sign, nearly there.

'This can't be right, the road has come to an end. We are at the sea wall! I'll ask this chap, excuse me have you any idea where Faraway Cottage is?'

'Yes Sir, that be it over there,' he said pointing out to sea to a wooden chalet on stilts.

'That can't be right, it's surrounded by water, how do you get there?'

'You use that dingy with *Faraway* written on it Sir.'

'I'm not going out there,' says Lyn, 'and that's final.'

'Well, let's just row out there and see if the keys fit, it might be the wrong place,' I say trying to keep things calm.

'OK, we will just look and that's all!'

'I shouldn't take those cases Sir, the dingy is only meant for two people. I'll give you a hand with it.'

So we get into the dingy and I row the few hundred yards to the cottage landing stage. No mistake, a big sign over the front door states *Faraway Cottage.*

'Come on Lyn, let's go in and have a look, might not be too bad.'

I open the front door to reveal a double bed to the left and a comfortable-looking sitting room to the right. Through the open door I can see a small kitchen. 'There you are, not too bad, let's just stay here tonight and we'll go home first thing in the morning. OK right.'

We lay on the bed and soon fell asleep to the sound of the water lapping underneath the cottage.

In the morning I wake to sun shining through the rooflight. I get up and look out the door. 'Lyn look, get up,' I shout, 'the water's gone. It's not the sea, it's a tidal river. We can walk ashore, come on!'

We walk the now-exposed footpath to the sea wall and the car. 'There's a shop over there, why don't I get some food, milk, etc and we'll have breakfast on the balcony?'

'OK,' says Lyn, 'seems a shame to waste the sunshine and this lovely view. I'll walk back and put the kettle on.'

'Morning,' says the shopkeeper, 'you be staying at Faraway Cottage then?'

'Yes,' I reply.

'You'll need one of these then Sir.'

'What's that?' I ask.

'A tide table Sir, £1.50.'

'Thank you.'

I walk back to the cottage and we have breakfast on the balcony overlooking the river boats going by, people waving. This is quite nice.

With the use of the tide table we manage to walk ashore to the pub and restaurant and we didn't use the dingy again.

In the evening we whiled away the time with bottles of wine sitting on the balcony into the early hours.

'That week went quick,' says Lyn as I lock the door and we make our way to the car. Lyn's driving. Not a word is said until we reach the motorway. 'Well so much for Faraway Cottage. That's an experience we'll never forget. So we're both agreed then, we'll book it again next year.'

THE DAY MY SHIP CAME IN . . .
G K (Bill) Baker

I must have been about twenty-five at the time. I know that it seems a hell of a long time ago, because I'm eighty now, but some things seem to stick in your mind forever and only surface when the occasion arises, as now!

I was, am and always will be, a keen sea angler and it was because of this that the events described as follows came to take place.

I was employed in those days by a local ship's chandler, a sort of general supermarket for the ships that came and went from Swansea in far larger quantities than they do today. It was our job to see that each ship sailed from the port with sufficient provisions to get them to their next port of call without running short of anything. No popping to the corner shop when you're a thousand miles from anywhere!

The entrance from the Bristol Channel to the Swansea docks was tricky to say the least. Only a narrow channel marked by 'fairway buoys' led up to the east and west piers and the River Tawe in-between and woe betide any largish ship that tried to cut costs by not employing a sea pilot to see them safely into the docks. A few yards either side of the channel and they would find themselves firmly embedded on the shoaling sands of Swansea Bay and it was a very costly business to employ tugboats to get themselves re-floated!

At the time we are talking of, The Swansea Pilotage Authority had a pilot cutter (or boat) named the Roger Beck, after a well known Swansea personality. This boat worked continually in three twenty-four hour shifts, using three separate crews, each with their own captain. It was the job of each captain to ferry out the sea pilots to the incoming ships and also to take off the pilots from the outgoing ships when they were safely in the Bristol Channel.

Naturally, it was mainly tidal work, as the bigger ships could only navigate when the high tide gave them sufficient water to carry them in!

One of the three Roger Beck's captains was named Hamilton, who lived at West Cross, a suburb of Swansea and as he obtained most of the stores from our ship's chandlers, we became quite friendly, resulting in an offer by him to take me out for the day so that I could do some fishing in Swansea Bay. A date was fixed and after signing over a sixpenny stamp to relieve the Pilotage Authority of all responsibility if anything should happen to me whilst on their boat, I eventually found myself anchored over the Green Grounds, a well known haunt of all types of fish eager to hook themselves onto my line.

This proved to be the case as, fishing with an old-fashioned three-boom brass paternoster, baited with lugworm dug from Swansea beach, I would lower the three-baited hooks to the sea bed where there was an immediate *bang . . . bang . . . bang*, as three eager to commit suicide fish impaled themselves onto my three hooks.

As fast as I could reel in and remove the fish, rebait and lower the line again, so would three more fish fight to get themselves hooked.

I had never experienced fishing like this before and soon had enough fish for myself, the captain *and* all the crew to have a tidy lot to take home for a fish supper!

All too soon it was time to up anchor and head for home. I'd no sooner managed to get my fishing tackle packed away than it was pitch-dark. From where we were, Swansea looked like fairyland with its millions of lights.

The captain invited me up to the wheelhouse for the return journey and from there gave orders for the anchor to be pulled up. He rang down to the engine room for the engines to be started up and soon we were on our way.

He pointed out to me the two pinpricks of red and green lights of the east and west piers, which at that distance seemed very close together. I could understand how imperative it was to stick to the fairway channel to avoid running aground. Though, being such a small ship compared with some of the huge ships that came in, we didn't expect to run aground.

I watched the captain handling the wheel and noted that, unlike a car, he turned the wheel left to go right and to the right to go left!

He turned to me and asked, 'Would you like to have a go?'

To which I answered, 'Oh, yes please.'

So he surrendered the wheel to me and showed me how to hold it and how to keep the ship steady.

He then said, 'I'm just going to make a cup of coffee in the galley. I won't be long. Just head straight between the red and green lights of the two piers and you'll be OK.' And with that, he left the wheelhouse.

So! There was I, in complete charge of a ship, albeit a small one, heading towards two pinpricks of light that were getting ever nearer in the pitch darkness of the night.

I must be honest, I was bloody terrified! Then I thought to myself, *The captain trusts me! I mustn't let him down! He won't let me put the ship at risk!* I was determined not to let him drown, so I put my fears on one side and concentrated on keeping a straight line towards the centre of the two pinpricks of light which were growing closer and ever closer.

Suddenly they were gone! I realised that we'd gone between the lights and were heading up the River Tawe towards the South Dock jetty where we were to tie up. We were doing a steady five knots, only a matter of three hundred yards from our destination, and still no sign of the captain or his bloody coffee!

With the odd light or two on the left bank giving some illumination, I could see the approaching jetty, and turned the wheel slightly to the right to come closer to the left bank, when the door opened and a voice said,

'Well done, Bill. I couldn't have brought her in better myself.'

Yes! It was the captain. He took the wheel and rang down to stop the engines. My ship had come in at last, and not only that, I'd actually brought her in myself!

Passing Through
Gardiner M Weir

He was standing outside the door of the pharmacy, dressed in a white dispensary coat, his hands clasped across his front. He looked up and down the village street as if to check who was about at that early hour of the morning. There was just me, cycling to a stop before him. He smiled as I approached and, anticipating that I was a customer, slipped back through the door into the shadows. He was already behind the counter as I entered. Again he smiled, this time accompanied by a slight lift of his brows, a professional expression that asked how he could serve me. I showed him my swollen hand.

'Ah!' he said. 'A bee sting?'

I confirmed his diagnosis and asked if he could do something to take away the pain. His expression changed to one of deep thought as he scanned the shelves of bottles that lined the walls. Then, in a matter of moments, he had taken one down and was applying a wad of cotton wool soaked in cooling liquid. I could feel the benefit immediately. I was impressed and sought to tell him so.

'You're a marvel!' I said happily. 'You're quite a genius!'

He drew himself up, grasped the air with one hand and claimed in theatrical tones, 'I,' there was a pause, 'am a chemist!' He leaned forward to look straight into my eyes as if to enforce my appreciation of that fact. Apparently I was not as influenced as he had expected for he continued in a more intense manner as if compelling me to understand. 'A pharmaceutical chemist, that is.'

He was a tallish, slim man of dark complexion with heavy eyebrows and a straight nose. His hair was brushed straight back from his forehead and gave him a remarkable resemblance to actors from the forties, a Charles Boyer. It seemed he thought so too and pronounced his words in a deliberate slow fashion, each one clearly enunciated as if reading from a script.

'You might say an apothecary!' he continued. 'A latter day Druid. Maybe even, you could say, a modern Merlin.'

There were many pauses for dramatic effect while his hands drew fantasies in the air.

By now I had accepted a chair. There I sat, in a low spectator's position, surrounded by his gallery of bottles of all sizes, shapes and colours. I could only nod my head before he was treading the boards again.

'You see, I dispense magic elixirs for the sick in body and potions and aids to guarantee and improve God's original handiwork and so,' there was a considerable arm flourish at this point, 'further the aims of the Devil!' He looked at me intently. 'That's a line I quote from the Reverend. He accuses me of being in league. You'll know him, I'm sure.'

I shook my head and told him I was just passing through on a cycling trip. It was really my first time in this village.

'Aye,' he continued as if I had not spoken, 'the good Reverend lives in a world occupied by God and the Devil!' He stared at me meaningfully and, with a deprecating smile, admitted, 'Not that I believe in either of those fabulous personages. Not me! No, not me! I... am a scientist! A scientist, you see.' He gave me a knowing wink. 'And that creates a conflict not easily resolved by simple faith. A question of the intellect!' He looked off into some distant part of his mind. 'And yet I deal in faith. For what is medicine, the greater part of it, but faith. And faith is in the mind.'

He reached forward to hold the wet compress to the back of my hand. I was his prisoner.

'Yes! I dispense the accoutrements of health and beauty to the sick of body and spirit and they have faith in me. In me! Yes! You know, when I think of it, the Good Lord,' he paused for several seconds,' that is to say, were He alive today, would make His mark as a pharmacist!' He looked at me to ascertain if I understood the significance of that pronouncement. 'Oh, if the scriptures had only read, 'They that are whole need not a pharmacist!' Wouldn't that be something! Dispensing aspirin and penicillin instead of barley loaves and fishes. What!' He leaned towards me with a wry smile. 'I once put that thesis to the Reverend, you know.'

I could only shake my head in astonishment.

'Aye! He was left without words! Now I'm a sinner, he says! A sinner! Doomed to the Fires of Damnation!'

I nodded my head silently. I had by now accepted my role. I kept quiet!

'He's either ignorant or stupid. Which do you think?'

'Who?'

'Thon shaman of a Reverend!'

I shrugged.

'The difference is this. Ignorance can be changed. But stupid! There's nothing you can do with stupid.'

Having made that point, the pharmacist posed a moment before a mirror that carried an advertisement for some effervescent fruit salts.

'Pharmacy, you know, is a wonderful profession!' he said to his image, sweeping his unbuttoned white dispensary coat in a wide swath. 'Once we were called apothecaries! Did I ever tell you that? I didn't, did I? He had strange intense grey-blue eyes that turned away to focus on some notion in the distance. 'You know I can repeat every word of the British Pharmacopoeia as if I had only qualified yesterday.'

'Goodness!'

'Just wait till you hear!'

And he began to recite incantations, ingredients, herbal cures and prescriptions.

I rose and, interrupting, asked him how much I owed for his services.

'Nah! It's nothing. Take care.'

He seemed to change character as an actor who has just left the stage. There was a look of hurt and disappointment on his face. I smiled to show I was not trying to offend him; just that it was time to go. I thanked him for his treatment of the bee sting. He grabbed my arm and looked at me intently.

'For in much wisdom is much grief: and he that increaseth knowledge increaseth sorrow.'

I could only stare at him.

'That's from Ecclesiastes.' He smiled deprecatingly with a downward tip to one side of his mouth. 'You know, young fellow, there's a lot of wisdom in the Good Book.'

At that moment there was a shadow in the light from the door and a man stepped in. He was dressed in black with a white clerical collar. The pharmacist stepped behind his counter, a smile once again on his face, his brows slightly raised to enquire how he could be of service. The Reverend laid a prescription on the counter top. I hesitated for a second, wondering how best to say goodbye, but he turned to me first. His face was blank of expression.

'Good day to you, sir.'

It was a beautiful sunny sky as I mounted my bicycle and road along the narrow street. I noticed the chapel with its stately spire and tall windows, its graveyard framed by stone walls, the weathered headstones. I continued my run through the back roads and lanes of the valley until I reached the high slopes of the mountain. Then I stopped once again, looking down the long incline, looking for the village in the distance that I had just passed through. It was sheathed in the foliage of trees with only the spire of the chapel to be seen.

BRAMBLES
Robert D Shooter

Delaying ordering the meal in 'Brambles' was one thing. Having finally ordered and eaten it, with a pot of tea to follow, and only half an hour to go before being back at work was another.

The idea to meet for lunch had been a good one - to support each other through the trauma. She could have been delayed? Maybe a crisis had occurred? My mobile was in my car. It was too hot to carry my briefcase and these white summer trousers didn't have a suitable pocket. Not like the dark ones with pockets everywhere. OK it could have been in my shirt pocket. I just didn't think I'd need it. Must be a moral there somewhere?

I was beginning to panic. Had she cracked up at work? Our daughter, Sarah, was seeing the doctor during the morning. Maybe he was nasty to her and Sarah needed putting back together in her mother's office?

There was now twenty-five minutes to work. I finished my tea and paid.

'If a stressed-out lady about my age but without grey hair comes looking for a stressed-out old man, say that I was here from 12.30 till now.' I realised the waitress looked puzzled. 'We arranged to meet here for lunch.'

'OK, Sir,' she said.

I came out feeling far more worried than when I went in. Something sinister must have happened. I couldn't just wander through the shops for a few minutes or beside the canal till work called, as I usually might. I had to settle what was wrong.

I walked to her office, guessing the way she might use, taking the main one. There were lots of others. But at her office she had booked out at 12.30pm and was expected back at 1.30pm; no crisis. Although in my heart, soul and stomach, there was an enormous one now. What happened in the few minutes between leaving her office and getting to the café?

Back in the heat of the day, I tried to think. I walked one of the other ways towards the café, but no clue. I tried using a public call box - I had my work diary with her mobile number, but it wouldn't register. It just cut out and gave me my money back. It was only later, when I was not panicking, that I wondered whether it was because a twenty pence was no use to call a mobile, and should I have put in a pound? But I was reeling now.

The news our daughter had given us was stressful. But she was robust enough. Determination to complete her degree and have the baby seemed likely to get her through, but us?

Should I go back to my office and phone her from there? What a stressful lunch! I walked back to 'Brambles' café.

'Has a lady like I described been in?'

'Oh yes,' they said in chorus.

My heart leapt with relief. Whatever had happened, she was OK. One said she'd come in a minute after I had left and then the other said five minutes.

I went to my car and switched on my mobile to ring her. Before I could, there were noises of texts and messages of missed calls.

One said, 'I am losing my marbles. I am sitting and eating in the wrong café. I'm in 'Atlantis'. I wondered where you were until now. I feel so silly. I'm losing it. Lost it. I've tried ringing you but your mobile is turned off.'

I rang her straight away.

'Where are you?' I ask.

'Back in my office.'

'I've just been there.'

'I know. Four different people have told me. I lost it.'

'I am so pleased you are OK. I thought something dreadful had happened. I won't leave my mobile another time!'

I heard her crying.

I said, 'I know I should be back at work in five minutes. But if I come over, have you time for a coffee? We need to support each other.'

I heard her laugh. Thank God for absurdity.

'Yes.'

CAROL'S PANDORA'S BOX
Carol C Olson

I was sitting inside our tiny cottage on a very hot and lazy summer afternoon.

I opened the brown box, tied with strings before me. It had been sent to me by a late uncle named Phillip. He was my father's only brother 6 years younger. Unbeknown to me, Uncle Phillip had been closely involved regarding family decisions in my very early years.

My father, Gustaf, was tall, dark, sultry, with a Valentinoesque look about him. During domestic difficulties, Gustaf turned to his younger brother, Phillip, for advice and counsel. This was one of the things I learned on reading some of the letters. In this brown box, besides letters, were pictures and other memorabilia that had been previously unknown to me. I was amazed at the pictures of a curly-haired toddler picking flowers in Grandmother's flower garden. Also others of me as a baby being held by both Mother and Father.

I continued as if in a fog, to read voraciously diaries that were kept by my father, his love poems to my mother and other writings. Little did I know when I opened the box what treasures lay inside for me to discover. Slowly, ever so slowly, it began to dawn on me that this was partly my story. It became very real to my heart . . .

Now I came to the packet of letters written in the 30s and 40s, when this wartime drama took place. Not only did I learn of my parents' marriage, but of what kinds of personalities and characters they had. These came shining through each page as though written with an illuminating pen! I learned things about my father, Gustaf, that I hadn't known. That in his 20s he and 2 other young men were tap dancers extraordinaire, with quite an act. Fred Astaire was my father's idol. The 3 guys danced in Vaudeville shows. In New York City at the Palace, and in Chicago, Gustaf was called 'Rubber Legs'. One of the fellas had an injury to his knee just as they were to meet with Mr Zeigfield's manager. This brought an end to the act. Gustaf went to work as a soda jerk in a small fountain in a drugstore close to home. Gustaf was also a pianist. He played so magnificently that people who heard him play were drawn to him like moths to a flame when he sat down at the keyboard.

Both of his parents had come from the old country in Sweden. I continued to read on, learning that my mother, Ingrid, had met my father at the soda fountain and attended youth meetings at a local church.

Ingrid's parents also came from Sweden. She was a gorgeous, auburn-haired beauty. She was so breathtaking to see that she won the 'Miss Iowa' beauty pageant in 1924 at 16 years. She then went on to business college and became a legal secretary. She also played the piano, was an artist in pencil drawing and a 'Romantic' . . .

When I first met my mother, having been separated since the age of 3½ years, I took her a perfect rose that I'd held in the plane for miles. The first thing I noticed, besides her angelic face and sweet spirit, was the gentle and soft voice and the grace when she walked. I could see right away why she had been picked as Miss Iowa years ago. I read on. Both she and my father had played twin pianos at home.

Gustaf had risen in a young and growing company. He became their office manager. He had a brilliant mind with figures and words. Soon he was sent to open other offices in large cities across the USA. It was altogether exciting for me to read about Gustaf and Ingrid and their adventures. It made me realise a bit more about myself through their writings.

The more letters I read, they began to beckon me to another time, the 2nd World War years. Insights came into their personalities and characters. Truly Mother and Father were *sensational* in so many ways.

Loneliness, stress, Gustaf's travelling without his wife, a wandering eye . . . marital difficulties came before the children.

A twist of fate found beautiful Ingrid, a pawn, vulnerable, with a husband tired of being tied down with a wife. A wife having post partum depression after giving birth to a little girl. The only answer given by husband, his mother and brother, Phillip was, 'Lock her up! Put her away! She's insane!' they all cried.

She was taken to the state mental hospital, and abandoned for 28 years. They put the little girl in an orphanage . . . where she spent 4 years.

Now dashing Gustaf became a merchant mariner. He played on shore at USO dances, not only the piano! He was spending time all over the world on an oil tanker as a pharmacist's mate and purser. His favourite places were Bora-Bora and Australia.

Reading all these letters over time, and rereading some, have certainly given me a new perspective and understanding, not only of my parents, but of the times when their little drama played out . . .

I have more questions and answers I'll not ever find. I became so immersed dwelling in all of the past, by all that was found in the brown box. I realised I didn't dare open it very often, or this box could become Pandora's box to me . . .

SLEEPING PARTNER
Jean Paisley

The mist swirled across the sand and the bell tolled slowly from the lighthouse warning sailors not to come too close. Black, slimy rocks peeped up from the waves like black widows waiting for their prey.

This was the day that they came up from the cold sea spray. Long metallic craft hovered above the sand. Bright lights searched the long, flat beach, white searchlights like long ghostly arms embracing everything that they touched.

They looked like us in silver radiation suits as they jumped down from their craft and landed on the golden sand. As they walked up through the town, people just gave them a glance and wondered what disco they were going to. No one even thought of ringing the police, after all, there were a lot, but people seemed to think that it was all just part of some business promotion. But, they stopped and put on their helmets that covered every part of their skin, this then caused a twinge of fear in people who had not been drinking as yet.

A young girl came out from one of the local pubs, she was staggering a little and kept on saying, 'Has anyone seen my car?'

The nearest man just extended his metal-clad arm, pointed straight at the girl and she was no more. She had just disappeared into the fresh sea air.

Some people ran into the bars warning people to stay off the streets. Everywhere these men in silver went, whole buildings disappeared Whatever took their fancy was just liquidated immediately and soon, where there had been a town, there was just an open space.

Fighter aircraft came out to meet the challenge, but these were sent into oblivion just like the young girl. Ships tried to launch a missile attack from the coast, but disappeared also. The perfect war machines had come to punish us. We never even heard them speak, we only saw them kill.

Where they had come from we didn't know. What did they want? The whole world without us on board. Other countries managed to send out a final code as they were taken too. At first the world was dusty for a while, but soon the sun shone on a forest shimmering in its light.

The new folk climbed out of their spacesuits. Some of them had blue skin that looked like satin, and they wore no clothes. Other people were green or brown. They seemed to worship the earth, rubbing the soil between their thumbs as though it were pure gold dust.

They used their craft fishing for octopus and squid while running around in the sunshine enjoying themselves. At least it seemed that way to a handful of people out there in space who lived upon the Mir Six. Watching Earth had taken on a different meaning now as Gregory said, 'I always knew that there was someone else watching us.'

'Yes,' said Ivan, 'unfortunately we were looking up into the sky most of the time.'

'The hollow Earth people were right all of the time, then,' said Ivan, 'there was another race right here on Earth.'

Gregory looked back at the screen and said, 'What a pretty woman, even if she is green.'

'Shall we blow the Earth up?' said Ivan.

'Maybe we should just observe them for a while first,' said Gregory.

'What's that on the communications network?' said Ivan. 'We never get code blue.'

Gregory sprang back into life dragging himself away from the many coloured delights of screen Earth.

'Someone is coming in from deep space in the region of Sirius Major,' said Ivan as he tried to make contact.

Then a very strange message appeared before their eyes. It read, *I am Moses and I am bringing back Jesus Christ.*

Ivan was stunned but he sent out his own message. *Earth is now populated with a new species and they are dangerous, we are the last men and women in space, only a few dozen aboard the spacecraft, Mir Six.*

And so, they came in glittering craft like diamonds above the Earth. Some beings flew in glass-like capsules and you could see their long, white robes. They lit up the sky with pictures of Christ and the Virgin Mary.

Back on Earth the aliens put on their silver suits. They began to fire their weapons but their rays bounced off the newcomers' spacecraft. The sky was lit up day and night, but still they would not give up the Earth. *You now have 40 days,* was written in the sky.

Later, when this time had past, bolts of fire were shot down into the sea. Huge oblong craft came to the surface bursting into flames. Tall pillars of fire consumed everything on land.

We waited for the time when the Earth would be renewed and the sun shone down upon us. The word came from the diamond craft that we could all go back. We climbed into our shuttles to start a brand new age. But, this time we would not be left with laser-written stone. A base would be set up and man would not be left alone.

APERTURE IN REALITY...
Cathy Stephens

I awoke with a start. *What the... where was I? How did I get here?* My mind was somewhat dulled and fuzzy as I tried desperately to remember what had happened. It was very dark and damp and I could feel the chill in my bones. I could make out contours of rocks and it looked somehow like a swamp I really must be dreaming... surely? I tried to check an injury I'd sustained, but apart from feeling cold and damp, I didn't think there was any real damage. Not seeing anything of clarity, I tried to focus; this didn't feel right or safe! I was too frightened to move! I was shivering but there seemed nothing around me.

Hot tears sprang from my eyes. I could feel my legs and arms but was totally mystified! There was a sound of dripping water and the sound of movement, perhaps something like a stream? I tried to gather my thoughts, I couldn't stay here; it was too dark and threatening! I began to feel very frightened! I tried to stand up as my eyes adjusted to the darkness. It seemed to be some sort of cave. I knew I had to escape! There was an aura of evil in the air. I tried to move but found my feet were stuck on the ground. My fear increasing, I found my voice to call out, 'Why am I here? Say something please if you can hear me... please... please?'

In the stillness I thought I heard some movement, yet I couldn't move, I was rooted to the spot! The stench became unbearable and I was struggling to breathe. *Oh, God, this must be Hell!* The movement was coming closer, I tried to close my eyes but I was transfixed to the shape in the water. Slowly it advanced, the stench getting stronger! I prayed! *Please let me be dreaming.* A second seemed like a minute, a minute like an hour! The shape stopped abruptly. It rose from the water yet still I couldn't see clearly. Minutes passed, I thought I was going to faint. I managed to grasp what seemed to be a jagged rock. I called again, 'Who are you? What do you want from me?'

Suddenly there was a sound from the creature, a rasping voice, ugly and vile, 'Come precious, you are mine now,' it seemed to be saying.
I desperately tried to move, to run, to flee from this place, but it was hopeless! I felt doomed. The reason I don't know, nothing seemed real.

There came a shaft of light illuminating the most sickening of creatures with red and yellow eyes. I couldn't quite make out just what I was seeing! It seemed to urge me to go forward, still I could not move. I tried to scream or shout, but my voice was silent. Such terror like I've never felt before! I silently began praying to all who had gone before. If I was dead, so be it! But I beg you please, help! I do implore! Over and over I prayed! Whatever this thing was, I'd fight it! My prayers became more frequent as I pleaded to my saviour. I fell to my knees and found that I had a voice, softly at the beginning, but gaining power and determination. I spoke with strength in my voice . . . 'Be gone, repulsive creature, I'll not venture to your side!'

Suddenly there was a sound of thunder! Everything around me began to shake; I heard the sound of rushing water and steam was rising from the murky darkness. I didn't know what was going on! There was a crash of rocks falling and suddenly there appeared a blinding white light! I tried to focus on what was happening. There appeared to be a great upheaval, many rocks falling, the steam rising with a deafening sound. I felt I was being pulled in both directions. I don't know how long it continued, but as I tried to shield my eyes, there were human voices screaming in my ears.

For a time I thought it would never end. I found my voice again, much louder than before . . . 'Stop, stop,' I shouted. 'If this is a battle for my soul, you most foul creature, be gone, my soul will never be yours! I have a family and friends! I will fight you tirelessly to the very end! So be gone, Satan, I will never succumb to your ways!'

The air was full of that terrible stench. After what seemed like an eternity, it suddenly became quiet. I tried to focus. but again, I felt very tired. All was still, the stench gone. I fell to my knees; it no longer felt cold. As I succumbed to the dark, I felt safe and comfortable.

I thought I heard voices as I tried to raise my head again. Terrible thoughts entered my head . . . just maybe I was dead! A strong grip clasped around my waist. The voices continued as I felt myself rise, the light becoming brighter. I tried to focus on what was happening! I thought I could see some of my family huddled in a crowd, and faces of friends clapping. I felt so very tired, so weary. I don't remember much after that!

I awoke in a bright environment in a strange bed. I tired desperately to clear my head. I was in hospital, bandaged and feeling sore. The doctor came to my side and said, 'You had a lucky escape. That well is very deep, you know!'

My head began to clear as I thought through what had happened to me . . . I had been out with my two dogs in the field in the woods. I'd let them off their lead to run around and didn't notice the old well behind me. One of the leads caught my ankle and somehow I toppled over into the well.

I had mixed thoughts as I lay in the hospital bed. Everything seemed so real as I drifted in and out of consciousness trying to fight the tiredness that my body had surrendered to. I glanced out the window in the hazy evening light. my thoughts swamped by the memory of my relatives and my dear husband standing side by side and smiling! Had I experienced a struggle between Heaven and Hell, or was it just the effects of the bang to my head? Perhaps one day I'll know for sure! In this moment in time, I don't know; if anything, what my experiences meant . . .

GYPSY BLESSING
M D Wyatt

The long-skirted, long-haired gypsy woman barred my way into the supermarket, she held out a sprig of white heather.

'You have a kind face, lady, won't you buy some lucky heather?' she coaxed.

Usually I refused to buy goods from shiftless people like gypsies, but that morning, being a bit short of money myself, I felt a wave of sympathy for the woman. I bought a sprig of heather.

'Thank you, lady, you will have a lucky day,' she said.

Because I was a regular worshipper at the local church, I thought it was expected of me to go to the church fete being held that afternoon. At the fete I quickly passed by the cake stall as I could see the prices of the goodies were too high for my slender purse. However, to show support for the church, I bought a twenty pence ticket for the tombola. On the tombola stall some nice prizes were on show, a tin of ham, a large box of chocolate biscuits and a basket of fruit. I hoped so much to win something nice to eat as Anna and Emily, my two little girls, would like a treat after their meal of baked beans on toast. It was my fate, though, to win an old, slightly chipped china piggy bank. *So much for the lucky day that the gypsy prophesied for me,* I mused as I trudged home.

Three o'clock chimed out from the clock in the church tower. That meant that my girls would soon be home from school, so I walked a little quicker. Just as I reached our front gate, it started to pour with rain; in my hurry to reach the shelter of the porch, I stubbed my toes on an uneven paving stone on the garden path. 'More good luck today, I don't think,' I muttered as I hobbled up the path, wincing at the pain in my toes.

I did not care much for the china pig, so I decided to put it on the top shelf of the dresser in the kitchen. As I am a fairly short woman, I stood on tiptoe to reach the high shelf, but a pain shot through my injured toes. I slipped and dropped the piggy bank on the tiled floor. I looked down to see the pig's head had smashed into several pieces and the body had broken in half. I angrily knelt on the floor to clear up the broken china. I picked up the rear end of the pig, and, to my surprise, saw inside it, folded up small, a twenty pound note! What a bonus, now I could buy the girls the much needed gym shoes and a large punnet of strawberries for a treat. It seemed the gypsy was right. It was, after all, my lucky day.

IF ONLY I WAS A MILLIONAIRE
F R Smith

If only I was a millionaire, I would have a car, a yacht and cash to spare. I would live in a marble mansion cool, with air conditioning and a swimming pool . . . and with lots of servants to wait on me . . . oh what a happy man I would be!

I was thinking such things as I was lying in my bed the other night - my eyes were closing and I was drifting gently into the land of *just supposing* when, just as sleep's dark arms embraced me, my alter ego emerged from the shadows to accompany me into the realms of fantasy.

In my dream, my day started, not with the strident summons of my alarm clock, but to the muffled swish of velvet drapes as a soft footed butler let in the light of day.

'Good morning Sir . . . your bath is prepared and breakfast will be served as soon as you are dressed. I have laid out your pearl-grey suit,' said the apparition deferentially.

I tried to focus my eyes in an effort to identify this smooth voiced stranger, but sleep was reluctant to loose its grip. Whoever he was, I liked his attitude. His melodic voice held a hint of grovelling reverence. Stretching luxuriously in my cocoon of silken elegance, I asked, 'What's it like outside . . . weather wise I mean?'

'Pleasant Sir - very pleasant indeed. One might even say, clement. Your coffee Sir.'

I rubbed my eyes. The man's image was still indistinct, but I fancied I could see more than a passing resemblance to my employer - except that my boss wouldn't give me the time of day, much less coffee.

'Good . . . in that case, I'll take a stroll in the park and on the way, I'll call at the bank . . . I need some money.'

As I approached the bank later, the manager came out on the steps to greet me and with a smile which threatened to bisect his face, opened the door and ushered me in. He led me through the assembled staff members, all bowing and applauding, towards the counter where an open briefcase stuffed with bank notes, was awaiting my collection.

'What's all this . . . what's going on? I didn't ask . . .'

'With the compliments of the bank Sir . . . a small token of our esteem.' The Manager bowed obsequiously.

I was confused . . . this wasn't the manager I knew . . . maybe the staff had been changed . . . I stared hard. This one too bore a strange likeness to my employer, though to be truthful, my boss was not over-practiced in the art of bowing.

'Ah well . . . in that case - thanks very much.' I said.

The manager's bow progressed to a cross between a curtsey and a grovel. 'Not at all Sir, you are more than welcome . . . and there is plenty more where that came from . . . you only have to ask!'

Picking up my case, I favoured the assembled staff with my interpretation of the regal wave and sauntered out into the afternoon sunshine.

On the street, I stood and thought for a while. What should I do? Here I was, loaded with money and at a loss to know what to do with myself . . . should I shop around . . . flash a few fivers? There's nothing more certain to get attention than throwing money about . . . and I needed attention. No one had taken much notice of me until now . . . my brow furrowed. I was in the position of being able to buy anything I fancied, but couldn't think of anything I wanted.

I wandered on aimlessly. Glancing at my watch I realised I hadn't had any lunch . . . 'There's that posh restaurant . . . I wonder what it's like inside?' I murmured.

The doorman, festooned with gold braid and looking more like a character from a comic opera than a door opener, greeted me with a smile, a smile which radiating from the corners of his mouth, threatened to join up again at the back of his neck as; he acknowledged the generous tip I pressed into his palm. He must have thought I was Father Christmas on early reconnaissance.

Inside, the lighting was so discreet as to be almost sinister. The head waiter moved to welcome me and escorted me to a damask covered table. At the imperious click of his fingers a white jacketed underling popped up at my side like Aladdin's genie released from his lamp.

'Would Monsieur care for an aperitif before ordering?' he asked, handing me a menu.

I did a bit of self preening - all this servility was doing my neglected ego a power of good . . . 'Yes . . . a scotch and soda will go down well.'

In seconds the waiter reappeared bearing my drink, then hovered wraithlike at my side . . . 'Whenever you are ready to order Sir . . . there's no hurry.'

Temporarily ceasing to hover, he ostentatiously shuffled the knives and forks.

That will be another fiver on the bill I shouldn't wonder . . . but what the hell, it's only money!

Sipping my drink, I took stock of the other diners. They were an opulent looking lot. Not surprising I thought, judging by the prices they charge here . . . the men were all smartly dressed - designer suits, collars and ties . . . no jeans or sweatshirts in this place . . . as for the ladies . . . they were either over or underdressed, depending upon how one viewed them . . . with some, décolleté bordered on the catastrophic. I continued to muse . . . 'They'll be the chaps' secretaries I suppose, or possibly with more interesting job descriptions . . . as for the men . . . probably some of the *fat cats* the media go on about . . . though to be fair, they don't come much fatter than me, or much cattier either . . . I wonder what they do for a living? They could be anything I suppose . . . bank managers - even bank robbers . . . who knows? Drug dealers or pushers . . . money launderers . . . chiefs in privatised industries, easing their stresses. Here's that waiter again - he's fiddling with the ashtrays now . . . I'd better order something I suppose.'

I studied the menu. Oh my God, it's one of those . . . why can't they write them in English, you'd know what you were getting then . . . they only do it to show off - pretending they're French or whatever . . . I can't understand a word of it . . . have to take a chance I suppose . . . I pointed to the card . . . 'I'll have some of this and a bit of that . . . and a bottle of this Chateau whatever . . . thanks!'

Minutes passed giving me time to resume studying my fellow diners. It looks as if a few have nodded off . . . got fed up with waiting, I shouldn't wonder . . . where's my lunch? They must be on a go-slow! Ah . . . at last!

With an exaggerated flourish, my meal was set before me. I rubbed my eyes in disbelief . . . meal? Is this it? I thought I had ordered food - there wasn't enough on my plate for one good sized bite. They say that a 'top chef' has to be something of an artist . . . if this is true, the one on duty here was a reincarnated Michaelangelo. It looked as if someone had merely added a little more to the plate's decoration. I'll bet there are no flies in the kitchens here - they're all dead from starvation . . . I wish I'd gone for a pub lunch now or that fish and chip shop in the High Street . . . that's food that is - not this fancy God knows what rubbish.

One thing's for sure, I won't come here anymore, millionaire or no millionaire . . . 'Waiter . . . bill please . . . let me get out of here.'

It felt good to be outside in the air again after the gloom inside the restaurant. If it had not been for the occasional clank of cutlery, one could have been in a chapel of rest.

Disappointed, I walked on. I looked at my watch . . . 3 o'clock and I had done nothing. How I used to long for time and money. There was so much I dreamed I would love to do, but now I had the time and could think of nothing. I could go to the cinema I suppose . . . it will pass the time . . .

I awoke . . . it was seven o'clock, I must have fallen asleep . . . I'm not surprised, the film was rubbish.

Feeling better after a burger and chips, I stared into shop windows to pass the time and lingered outside a travel agency . . . some of these brochures look really interesting, judging by the photos. I could do with a holiday myself . . . somewhere exotic, away from it all - with lots of sand and sun and sea . . . yes, I'd like that . . . just look at all those bikini-clad beauties . . . cor! But, they're clever, these tour operators . . . they never tell the whole story - there's always a downside to their 'never to be repeated' offers. They never mention sub-standard lodgings or salmonella, typhoid, diarrhoea, flies, fleas and all the other bugs and pests with which you share their earthly paradise. They don't show those on the brochures do they - little things like that they just ignore. They should advertise the reality of their short breaks - two weeks without a care, followed by a few months of intensive care. It's not for me, I'll do my holidaying via the telly. I don't need any 'wish you were here' - I can wish myself anywhere.

I wandered on. If I had thought of it earlier, I could have gone to the races. Not that I could get much pleasure watching bookmakers pocketing my money. Betting's a mugs' game and I find the contrast between the beauty of the racehorses and the sad lack of it in their seedy looking owners, depressing to say the least. If I could watch the owners galloping around the track for a bag of oats, that would be worthwhile.

Another thought struck me. I have never been to a night-club. I've often wondered what goes on in there . . . it could be interesting . . .

Well here I am inside. It's a strange sort of place - has an atmosphere all of its own . . . a mix of excitement and anticipation . . .

there's depression too . . . even fear . . . it's a curious cocktail of emotions - principally greed!

I strolled around the gaming rooms. A low buzz of conversation harmonised with the click of counters, the flick of cards and the clatter of the little white ball as it leapfrogged its crazy way over the hurdles on the roulette wheel. I heard the gasps and shouts of the winners when it came to rest and the groans of those who had lost. I studied the faces of the croupiers as they raked in a small fortune after every spin of the wheel - expressionless - dispassionate . . . well, it was only money after all and it wasn't theirs anyway.

This is not for me . . . a waste of time and space . . . 'I'm getting out of here,' I said.

It was dark outside as I started home. As I walked along, I saw a figure coming at me from out of the darkness and a finger of fear touched me.

'Hi ya guv . . . how about a wet for an old sweat?'

I backed away - the man was not alone. Others were closing in - ghoulish figures emerging from the shadows . . . a whole procession with outstretched arms . . . some waving banners, bearing down like a flotilla of tall ships under sail . . . line abreast they came, shouting, screaming, pointing . . . menacing . . .

Grasping hands, ugly and ham-like, other skeletal with talon-like fingers . . . reaching . . . faces, twisted with greed and spilling hate thrust into mine . . . I was backed against a wall . . . I couldn't move . . . there was no escape. In blind panic I opened the briefcase and threw its contents, like confetti, to the wind . . . notes flew in all directions.

'Take it . . . take it all and leave me alone!' I screamed and turned to run, leaving the ugly 'free for all' behind me. A hand touched my shoulder . . . 'Aaaaaaah . . .'

'Fred . . . wake up . . . what's the matter . . . are you alright?'

Bathed in sweat, I opened my eyes and looked into my wife's concerned face. Shaking with relief, I took her into my arms and embraced reality. 'Yes darling, I'm alright now.'

'You had a bad dream dear, that's all.'

'No darling, I had a nightmare. I dreamt I was a millionaire.'

KEEPING UP APPEARANCES
Rosemary Pooley

Florrie was unpacking when she heard a knock at the door. She opened it with a ready smile on her face and found herself looking up to a tall, bottle blonde woman, whose smile did not reach her eyes. 'Hello,' the woman drawled, 'I'm Angela Ponsenby, your neighbour.' She slowly extended a slender brown arm, nails freshly manicured, fingers adorned with expensive rings.

Looks as if she hasn't done a day's work in her life, thought Florrie as she held out her own chapped hand, revealing ragged nails. Their hands touched for a second, then Angela hastily drew hers away. 'I'm Florence.' Florrie used her best telephone voice but it didn't match Angela's posh tones by a long shot.

Angela looked Florrie up and down. A sarcastic smile twitched at the corners of her mouth. Florrie felt the back of her neck prickle. Flippin' cheek, she was only 45 and on close inspection Angela wouldn't pass for much less!

'How are you settling in?' Angela raised a carefully plucked eyebrow as she took in the mess on the floor.

Nosy so and so Florrie thought. Well it wouldn't do to fall out with the neighbours on the first day. She and Derek had agreed to leave their old lives behind them and try and 'fit in'.

'Coffee?' Florrie stepped back, bumping into a box. She turned and triumphantly plucked the coffee jar from amongst the shoes.

'Oh, instant.' Angela licked her lips as if there was something nasty on them. 'Actually, I think I'll decline.'

Well, the cheek of the woman, you'd think she'd been offered dishwater! Florrie shut the door and looked in the mirror. No wonder Angela had looked at her like that. Her hair was a mess and her tracksuit had seen better days. Well, she'd just have to get on with it. She had expected to be out of her league but she couldn't begrudge Derek his promotion and transfer, especially as it meant she could give up her job at the meat paste factory. She would just have to make an effort.

The next day Angela came round again. 'I'm having a fondue party this evening, would you like to come?'

'Ooh, one of those French farewell parties you mean? I've never been to one - yes please.'

Angela smirked. 'Oh dear, you really don't know what I mean do you?'

Florrie felt her nostrils flaring. 'Actually, I've just remembered, I'm going out this evening.' She shut the door as firmly as she dared without actually slamming it.

That evening over tea, Derek asked, 'Are you alright love? You've been very quiet since we arrived.'

'Oh Derek,' Florrie felt the tears begin.

Derek pushed his plate aside and beckoned Florrie onto his lap for a cuddle.

'It's that woman next door, I've tried to be friendly but she looks down on me. I feel so fat and frumpy compared to her.'

'Mutton dressed as lamb if you ask me,' Derek replied. 'Anyway, I like my women with a bit of meat on them, not all skin and bone like her. Don't worry pet, I reckon it'll sort out in the end.'

Florrie glowed. Her Derek always knew what to say.

A few Angela-free days later, Florrie bumped into her outside the chippy. 'Hello Angela, fish and chips for tea?'

'Certainly not, we don't eat that rubbish!' Angela turned on her heel and marched off.

That night, cuddling up to Derek, Florrie started thinking. She tried to find out more. 'Angela's husband works at your place doesn't he? What's he like?'

'I don't really have anything to do with him, different department. I have heard that he is a bit of a ladies' man.'

'Ooh, poor Angela. You know, she spends a lot of time alone and I don't think many people went to her party the other night. I wonder if she is just putting on a show to impress me.'

'Maybe, don't worry about it love, come here and give us a cuddle.'

For the next few days all was quiet on the Angela front. The curtains were closed most of the time and Angela didn't go out.

'Guess what?' Derek burst out when he returned from work one day. 'I've discovered that your favourite neighbour hails from the same part of town as us and we know her old man - Doug Jones.'

'Doug the milkman?'

'Yes,' Derek grinned, 'don't you see, she is no better than us, she's just pretending to be posh and as for that husband of hers, well he's seeing my secretary at the moment from what I hear, so life is far from perfect. What's the matter love? I thought you'd be pleased.'

Florrie sat down, resting her chin thoughtfully in her hands. 'How can I be pleased Derek, I feel really sorry for her. Don't you realise that if I had carried on trying to 'fit in' like we agreed, I'd be like that eventually. I should thank her for stopping me.'

Florrie came up with a plan. She marched up to Angela's front door and knocked loudly. Angela opened it wearing an old dressing gown and no make-up.

'Angie love, we didn't get off to a very good start did we? I'm sure we can be friends if you'd like to give it a go. Get yourself dressed up for 7 o'clock and I'll take you out.' Florrie turned and hurried back home before Angela could answer.

Florrie did her hair and put on a bit of lippy, then nipped back to Angela's. Angela was ready. She smiled weakly and walked quietly with Florrie to the bus stop.

When they arrived Angela held back. 'Florrie, I'm not sure if I can, I mean, I don't think I want to . . .'

'Angie, where have you been, great to see you!'

Florrie hardly had time to find out who was talking before others joined in the greeting, crowding round and sweeping them to a table. Florrie quickly spotted some of her old pals.

'Florrie,' Angela gulped, 'thank you for being my friend, can we call a truce?'

'Of course,' Florrie smiled, 'now be quiet or we'll miss the start.'

A man's voice blared out, 'Good evening everyone, welcome. Now eyes down for the first game!'

THE COLOUR OF MOZART
Jonathan Attrill

Ellie loved listening to the paintings of Mozart. She sat back in her armchair with her headphones on and pressed the CD button. The beautiful, vibrant colours began to fill her soul. She loved the classics. From the light and happy colours of Boccherini's *Minuet* to the sombre, purples hues of Beethoven's *Moonlight Sonata*; from the kaleidoscopic concertos of Bach, where colours danced across the canvas of her imagination with notes that almost dazzled her with their brilliance, to the soft, pale blues and violet of Chopin.

She liked other painters, too. Other kinds of painting. Like jazz, with its experimental, improvised splashes of colour; rock, with its hard, clear, primary tones of blue, red and yellow; and the blues with its myriad shades of that colour - it was a pity other people didn't seem to know just how many shades of blue there were in the world.

She closed her eyes and relaxed as Mozart's colours washed over her. She'd even bought herself a guitar a couple of years ago, so she could mix her own colours. She wasn't much of a painter herself but she had learned a few chords and she enjoyed playing with the colours. 'A' minor was her favourite - a haunting indigo blue, dark and mysterious. Her mother had an indigo voice. She used to sing her to sleep with that colour when Ellie had been a child. Her father's voice had been a strong, deep crimson 'E', which had faded slightly with age to a mature burnt sienna. The 'A' major chord was a clean yellow, whereas 'C' was orange, like the fruit but slightly darker. 'G' was green - she'd never been that keen on the colour green but this was a nice emerald, like the colour of grass. When she played the guitar she loved hearing the different colours, especially the way they melted into each other when she changed chords; the resonance of one colour fading into the next like the sounds of the sunset.

Sunsets made such a beautiful sound. Those melancholy strings of dark blue, pink and purple, shifting and flaring, and then that final piercing crescendo of orange-red erupting across the sky in a final cry of despair, before dying in silence. Stillness. The sound of night. Then the metallic twinkling of the stars would begin, like a wind chime jangling in a gentle, evening breeze. Shortly joined by the harp of the moon, trembling its silver notes against the silent sky.

As a child, they'd said she was strange. The girl who could see the colour of sounds. Her parents thought she was just an imaginative child, but that was just the start. At about the age of seven she started to hear colours. She thought the rainbow made the most harmonious sound in the whole world. It sang in her head like a choir of angels. By then her parents knew there was something wrong. There had to be something wrong because everyone said so. She didn't see things the way everyone else did. Nor hear things the same. Nor even, by the age of twelve, taste, feel or smell things in quite the same way. Though they loved her dearly, her parents were forced to admit that their child was damaged.

They took her for some tests at the hospital. They called it synaesthesia; said they had never seen a case like it - but they could find nothing physically wrong. In fact, she was in perfect health. Therefore, said the doctors, it had to be psychological. So she went to see a child psychologist. He was a funny man, with a big, bushy beard and wild, curly hair. That was how she remembered him now, anyway. He asked her lots of strange questions. About her mum and dad and how she felt about them; about her friends at school - though by that time she didn't have many left because they thought she was a freak (although she suspected there was no little envy of her strange abilities). And about sex. He was certainly interested in sex. Aren't they all?

But with her it really was as fascinating subject. Even more so as she'd grown up and started having sexual relationships with men. It was interesting because during sex, at least the good sex, her senses didn't just swap or get mixed up. They merged. All of them. Sometimes, during orgasm, as she tasted the tang of unsweetened strawberries, she really did see something like fireworks going off and hear some kind of fanfare. Could you believe that? Sometimes, if she screamed with pleasure, it was almost hysterical because she was laughing at the same time at the sheer corniness of it. But there was all the other stuff before that. Like when Gerry, her first proper long-term boyfriend, had touched her - the way he'd touched her, on the neck and shoulders - it tasted of minty ice cream, with just a hint of chocolate chip. Whereas James' kisses had tasted of lemon sherbet and James hadn't had lemon sherbet since he was a child.

And talking of food, didn't chicken taste awfully prickly? She got prickles all over her when she ate chicken. Fruit, generally, was soft against her skin, but not as soft as chocolate. Dark chocolate made her feel like she was wrapped up in a soft blanket on a cold night. She loved the feel of chocolate. She could still taste it, the way normal people did, but sometimes it lacked something. That was the way it worked, the stronger the abnormal sense the duller the normal one and vice versa.

Sometimes she longed to be normal, to feel and touch and smell the way other people did. And there were times when she did precisely that. When she tasted food, heard sound and saw colours. But when she had a long spell like that she became afraid that she would lose her special senses and longed for them to return. They always did.

The most frightening times in her life, though, were when the opposite happened. When her 'super senses', as she liked to think of them, became so powerful that they blotted the others out altogether. Usually it was the colour or hearing sense that went into overdrive, the ones that had developed earliest and remained the strongest. During such intense periods she might become blind, deafened by the piercing sound of the sky or, if it happened when she was out shopping, the vast array of singing, clanging colours all around her. At such times she had to call her friend, Miriam, who would drive her home and tuck her up in bed so she could sleep it off. Those times never lasted long, yes, they were frightening times but, can you imagine, to be able to hear the sky! To be able to see the sound of laughter! Laughter was a truly beautiful, almost indescribable colour.

The best periods were when her senses were in perfect balance - half and half. Like this evening. Then she had the best of both worlds.

Her Mozart came to an end as the colours faded and disappeared. Ellie took her headphones off and looked at her watch. Almost seven-thirty. David would be home from work any minute. She got up from the chair and walked to the drinks cabinet. She made David a whisky and poured herself a glass of wine from the new bottle of Chablis she'd bought. She took a sip and smelt the flavour - orchids. She heard a key in the door and waited for the words he always spoke when he got back in the evening.

'Ellie, I'm home, darling!'

God, she loved the colour of that man's voice.

HORROR OF HORRORS
Ray Foxell

Frank lived on his own.

In the five years since his wife died there had been no great changes, only little ones. Things like his eyesight getting worse, and mowing the lawn becoming more and more of a burden, and having to give up golf, then the car. There was a married daughter, but she lived three hundred miles away and the relationship, never particularly strong, had deteriorated gradually to a card and a brief note at Christmas and on his birthday.

There'd been nothing much the matter with Mavis; no long, lingering illness, no sudden catastrophe like a car smash or a burning house, just a week of feeling 'under the weather', as she put it, then death. They'd been married for forty-one years and it had often surprised him, thinking about it since, how quickly the time had passed and how little he knew her. They'd had a comfortable if unexciting marriage and he wondered now what they'd found to talk about.

Financially, there were no problems. He'd joined the company straight from university and ended up on the Board. They'd given him a handsome golden handshake when he retired and the pension was more than most men get working full-time. The mortgage was long since paid off and anything he wanted, he could buy - painlessly. In fact, the house was full of gadgets they never used. Or rather, *he* never used. Funny how you can't quite get used to being on your own. Lovely house it was too. Detached, large garden, smart area.

'Money doesn't make you happy,' a friend had said to him years earlier, 'but you can at least be miserable in comfort.' That just about summed it up - miserable in comfort.

Frank had time to think about things he'd never considered when he was chairman of the Art Society, when there was a job to go to, a family to support, functions at the golf club, a busy social life. And all the cultural pursuits that seemed so meaningful and fulfilling twenty years ago had lost their appeal. The thrill of selling his first painting was a distant memory. He never got his paints out these days. What was the point? His failing eyesight made reading a problem and television not much better. His was a life of quiet desperation, waiting for the end and wondering what, if anything, it was all about.

Friends still dropped in though, from time to time. One of these was Harry. Harry was a year or two younger than Frank, a colleague from work before he took early retirement, affable, courteous, rather shy. They chatted for a while but Frank could see that this was more than a casual visit. 'Out with it, Harry. You've come to tell me something, haven't you?'

Harry seemed relieved that it was being made so easy for him. 'Yes, I have as a matter of fact.'

Frank smiled at his friend's embarrassment. What followed had obviously been prepared:

'Supposing I had some terrible disease, say, cancer. Death was certain and not far off. And supposing I discovered a cure and healed myself. And supposing I then took the formula, locked it away somewhere safe and never mentioned it to anyone. Wouldn't you say that was a criminal act?'

Frank nodded and smiled again, the sort of smile you use to humour and encourage someone.

'Yes, well, I've been healed of something a million times worse than cancer.'

Frank raised an eyebrow, this time without smiling.

'And it would be criminal of me not to tell you about it.'

'Go on, then.'

'Sin.'

'I beg your pardon?'

'Sin. Unfashionable word, eh? Taboo subject.'

'So what about it?'

'Whoever sins will die.'

'What are you talking about? Whoever *doesn't* sin will die. We're all going to die. You don't have to tell *me* that. Ever since Mavis went . . .'

'Sorry, Frank, I didn't mean to be insensitive, but there are two sorts of death.'

'Two sorts? Who says?'

'The Bible says.'

'The Bible?'

'*Everybody* has done wrong. We've all blown it. We all deserve to die . . .'

'But we're all *going* to die - I've just said that.'

'Not permanently.'

'What's that supposed to mean?'

'If you can find somebody totally innocent, willing and able to die the death *you* deserve . . .'

'Who says I deserve it? The Bible?'

'Yes.'

'Charming.'

'If you can find someone to die in your place, then you can go free and death has no hold on you.'

'That's a big 'if'.'

'It is, isn't it.'

'Got anyone in mind?'

'Yes. Jesus Christ. Look Frank, this is the formula - and I was thirty-five before I discovered it - he's done it all, come to this Earth, got involved in all our misery, all the mess, never put a foot wrong, died an appalling, agonising, cruel death, came back to life . . .'

'Came back to life? You're kidding.'

'No I'm not. He's still around. I've met him.'

'What?'

'Yes.'

'What did he look like?'

'It's not like that.'

'What's not like that?'

'You can't see him, but if you've got a relationship with him you can enjoy his company, know what he wants you to do, talk to him . . .'

'And does he talk to you?'

'Sometimes. Through the Bible mainly, but in other ways, too. In fact, I believe he told me to come here and speak to you today.'

'Good grief.'

'Look Frank, this has turned out rather like I was afraid it might, but I'm going to tell you something else. You know I said, 'supposing I had cancer?' Well, I *have* got cancer. The doctor's given me four, five, maybe six months.'

'Harry, I'm sorry.'

'No, it's all right. It really is. I'm not looking forward to dying, but I'm not frightened of death. And it's given me the courage to take the Formula out of the cupboard and show it to you. I expect you think I'm some sort of a nutter, but that doesn't matter anymore. I know I'm on my way to Heaven where there'll be no more crying, no more pain, no disease, no problems, no death. In fact,' he smiled for the first time, 'it'll be Heaven.'

'No offence Harry, but how do you know you're going to Heaven? I mean, what have you done to deserve that?'

'I haven't *done* anything, and I *don't* deserve it - it's a free gift.'

'Free gift?'

'Free to me, yes. But it cost Jesus his life. All *I* did was acknowledge the mess I'd made of everything and ask him to take over. And he did. And very gradually things have changed.'

'You? Made a mess of everything? I don't believe it.'

'Ah, but you didn't know the real me. He does.'

'This is all a bit sudden, you know. I've never been religious.'

'Great. Don't start now. Religion is a dead thing of dogma, ritual, ceremony, rules. Don't get religious. What you need is a love affair with the King of Kings.' He smiled again, rather sheepishly. 'Sorry, bit of jargon crept in there.' Frank smiled, too. This was a side of Harry he'd never seen before.

'And if you don't accept his offer of everlasting life, d'you know what the alternative is, the *only* alternative?'

'You tell me.'

'Everlasting torture. Hell. It's a place of utter darkness, *outer* darkness where people, *fully conscious,* are excluded from all that's bright and beautiful, where there's weeping and gnashing of teeth. Weeping because of all the misery and pain and suffering and hopelessness. Gnashing of teeth because of all the remorse, the if-only factor, the finality of it all. And the fire that torments you never goes out and yet you're not consumed, and the worm that bugs you, that's eating at you inside, will not die - it's there forever. And the screams of those around you in the blackness will make things even worse. They can't help you, they wouldn't want to, anyway. They have their own problems. And you can't look forward to death, when it'll all be over - that was the *first* death. This is the *second* death and it goes on and on forever and ever. This has to be the ultimate horror. Appalling, unspeakable, unimaginable horror.'

'That was very dramatic, Harry. And your god, is he a god of love?'

'Yes.'

'So why would he condemn anyone to Hell - all that gnashing and screaming?'

'He doesn't condemn anyone. In fact, he's done everything possible for us to avoid it. He sent his son Jesus to die the death *we* deserved. Beyond this, God cannot go. If you don't accept that, you condemn yourself. There's no halfway house between Heaven and Hell, no middle ground. It's one or the other.'

The conversation petered out after this. Harry sensed a barrier between them, an awkwardness which would not have been there if they'd been talking about the weather or the football results.

'Well, I must be going. I promised Jean I'd be back for tea. I think she wants to make the most of me.'

In the event though, it was Frank who died first. Harry went to the funeral a very sick man and he knew in his heart, beyond any doubt at all, that his friend had *not* taken hold of the lifeline he'd been offered.

For Frank then, the ultimate tragedy, the horror of horrors, had begun.

A STORMY NIGHT
Claire Caple

I blinked. Another boom rang out across the sky. I stopped walking and turned my face upwards. I saw a flash of light from somewhere amongst the clouds and a few drops of rain fell on my face. I had not noticed how quickly the clouds had gathered. Even as I thought this, the rain was rapidly becoming heavier and a fork of lightning struck the ground precariously close to where I was standing.

I lowered my head and pulled up the hood of my coat, wrapping it more closely around me. I shivered in the sharp chill wind, which seemed to freeze my bones to the marrow. My teeth chattered slightly at every gust.

I scanned my surroundings, frantically searching for somewhere that I could take shelter. There were a few trees scattered here and there in the fields, but I realised how foolish it would be to use a tree for shelter in the midst of a lightning storm.

Then my eyes fell on a dilapidated building standing on a low hill nearby. I paused for a few moments to consider the possible consequences. I could just imagine my mum warning me, 'Never, ever go in that house on the hill by Jack Randall's fields, Chloe. That place could be dangerous! It ought to have been knocked down by now!' Yet even as I remembered my mum's words, I came to the conclusion that, due to the present circumstances, it would be most sensible to take shelter inside the house.

Decided, I sprinted across the nearest field and up the hill to the dreaded building.

As I ran under the archway to the house's garden, I slowed to a halt and glanced around at the disorder. The garden was overrun with weeds that choked the only half-dead plants that grew there. Moss fought its way over the top of this growth and up the walls of the abandoned house. This bleak sight was rather deterring, but, as another rumble of thunder filled my ears, I was given no other choice. Gathering the little courage that I had, I rushed up the garden path to the front door of the house. As I pushed it open, it groaned on its single rusted hinge.

Then I stepped inside . . .

My heart pounded high in my throat as I entered the current object of my fear. The wind howled through the eaves of the house and I could faintly hear water falling in through a leak in the roof somewhere. I jumped with fright as the door suddenly slammed behind me. When I discovered what it was, I closed my eyes and took a few deep breaths. It was a futile attempt to calm my nerves.

After a few seconds, I walked further into the house. My eyes looked around and I caught sight of masses of cobwebs clinging to the walls and roof. I gulped and shivered, this time not completely because of the cold. I *hated* spiders.

Then a scuttling noise came to my attention. I listened carefully and it stopped. Then I heard it again. *Just rats,* I thought, trying to give myself a rational explanation. I also hated rats, but it was better than not having any idea of what it could be.

The sound seemed to come from everywhere at once. It surrounded me as I continued to step slowly across the floor, in the general direction of a flight of stairs.

All of a sudden, something creaked above me. The scuttling ended abruptly. A clap of thunder vibrated through the house. I glanced back at the door swinging on its hinges and saw a fork of lightning streak across the sky.

I had stopped in my tracks, but now I continued towards the stairs. Though the icy fingers of fear still gripped at my heart, I strangely felt extremely curious. This feeling was stronger than ever before, to the point that it was overpowering. It tugged me towards the stairs, which I began to ascend with barely another thought. Before I knew what I was doing, I had climbed to the top of the staircase and was looking across a landing.

I stepped forwards almost zombie-like, the rotten floorboards creaking in protest under my feet. A banister that used to be white, but barely had any paint left on the wood, was stood to my right. There was a wall along my left, with two doors that looked like they were about to collapse. At the end of the landing was a single solid-looking door. This was where I was drawn to like a magnet.

It was then that my mind caught up with me.

I blinked a few times and noticed something quite suddenly. I do not know why I thought of it then, but I had a good reason to. The lack of dust was what was so surprising. The house was antiquated, and should have contained much of it, but there was not a speck to be seen. My movements did not bring up clouds of dust from the floor, as I would expect them to. Another point was that I was not wheezing, which large amounts of dust caused, due to my asthmatic problems.

Without any warning at all, my foot suddenly fell through the floor. I managed to catch myself on a stronger set of floorboards, but not before my knee had already gone through the hole. I gasped when a pain shot up my leg. I dragged myself out of the gap in the floor and found a deep scratch half way down my leg. My trousers had been torn to expose the flesh, which was bleeding. Remembering something I had seen on TV, I ripped off the bottom half of my other trouser leg and tied it over the cut. It covered it mostly and slowed the flow of blood.

I listened very carefully and discovered that the storm had ebbed slightly. It would probably have been safe enough to go back outside again. Maybe it would have been better if I had done. I still had the feeling of intense curiosity, though.

I stood up and limped the final few steps to the single door. I reached out a shaking hand and grasped the cold metal handle. It moved under my fingers without any pressure at all. I snatched my hand away and the door swung open with an ominous groan. I moved forwards into the room and the door slammed shut behind me. I turned and tried to open it again, but it was stuck fast. I was trapped with no way out of a room in a dilapidated building.

A creak came from behind me. I spun around and put my back to the door. I could see nothing in the complete darkness. There were no windows to reveal whether or not something was lurking in the shadows. I bit down so hard on my bottom lip that I almost drew blood.

I waited for something to happen.

Something watched me from within the blackness.

And then it pounced.

I still could not see anything. I may as well have had my eyes closed. For a brief moment, I smelt its putrid odour. I felt it land upon me.

I screamed . . .

And woke up.

I sat up suddenly in my bed. The quilt fell from my shoulders and I was washed over by a great relief. Then I felt the pain in my leg, and I uncovered it.

There was a long scar halfway down my leg, as though from a deep scratch . . .

TITANIC IN ICE
FAC

The haunted iceberg wept icicles, she had to justify her years of drifting aimlessly. She knew her own kind could not care less where time and temperature changes took them, but she, though so gargantuan, felt as small as a pinhead, and could not rest. Ever since she had sunk 'the ship that even God could not sink', Titanic, the great white iceberg had known no peace. Because of her stress, she was becoming smaller, splitting, cracking and losing bits of herself, gradually disappearing, she was thus determined that whilst she had the size and strength left in her, she wanted to and must rescue Titanic! As she neared the scene of her crime, at last, trying to avoid other seafarers, and her own stubborn relatives, and passing acquaintances en route, her gigantic form trembled. A distant familiar place was appearing through the white gloom which she never thought she would ever have the courage to face again. Her solid mass experienced terrible alternative emotions of both panic and agitated excitement.

Her rock-solid base sensed something strange, a feeling of warmth emanating from the forgotten depths where Titanic lay. A bubbling and a gurgling with strange explosions and shudderings, causing her to begin melting, thus making space for the rusting sleeping giant, when to her utter amazement, an undersea volcano chose just then to erupt and force upwards shoving violently the enormous liner.

Now the combination of these four Herculeans the sea, iceberg, volcanic outburst and Titanic herself, fighting with one another was spectacular. It was as if the sea itself was being swallowed and going down some great plughole, whirlpools, corkscrews and funnels of the glacial liquid were turning the whole area for many miles around into a maelstrom of extraordinary activity. The enormous energy forces discharging themselves through the waters were terrifying:

... 'Reservoir of tears therein submerged screaming in silent agony,
Men's torn souls trapped there for infinity!
Taunting man in mists and fogs, salt water calling salt blood.
Affinity drawn on, drawn in, human bait lured,
Ultimate sacrifice, bone and flesh, swallowed and crushed
                                                    by the water,
Superman, never, he cannot compete with this stuff of life,

The sea our metre our womb of strife.'

(This must have been how it was at the beginning of time, only included now amongst the natural elements, was this huge extravagant ship.) The noise and commotion appeared on radars far and wide. The excitement mounted as people realised, just where the pandemonium was occurring. Before anyone could be there though, the sea divided and gave birth to a sight to outdo all sights: 'Titanic in ice!' The boiling fury of the volcano sent the iceberg at super speed cutting through the waters like a razor.

More and more of the weird apparition appeared thrusting onwards, creating speed through its own momentum. Helicopters arrived overhead, like angry mosquitoes zoom lenses and camcorders at the ready. The whole scene was quite spellbinding.

Iceberg laughed icicles now, somehow she knew that her age old victim Titanic, entrapped within her frozen hulk would have man's help to guide her to The White Star Line's berth at New York. Although she also knew her own mass would be claimed by the warmer seas through which she would pass, she realised man's technology would treat Titanic with incredible tenderness.

Long live leviathans with hearts and minds.

COLOURING THE TRUTH
Margaret Green

If I had known the outcome, I would not have taken the 8.25 train to Bolverton that sunny August morning, only I had a dental appointment to repair a back tooth cavity. The train had been standing on the platform as I purchased my ticket, but there were only two ahead of me, and without noticing who had joined the queue behind, I hurried to climb aboard. Considering what happened afterwards, things might have been different, but at the time I was intent on making the journey. It had been one of those compartment only carriages, and it wasn't until I'd become seated, that I saw John Carter, of Timms and Carter Solicitors, nodding and smiling, as one does when surprised at seeing a familiar face, and when Mathilda Underwood joined us, I quite looked forward to the journey, through what had become a rather mundane route. I never learned to drive you see nor yet wanted to. Somehow in my addled way I've always considered it a male prerogative, as my husband loved to slip behind the wheel. Such a dependable man my Henry, but I digress.

I'd lived in Cragdale as a child. A charming Derbyshire village, no more than a scattering of pale, stone-built houses, with a main street, a combined shop and post office, the church of St James, a junior school, and a couple of outlying farms. Just a hamlet really, surrounded by rolling fells, and dry stone walled plots, where cattle and sheep roamed freely in the verdant enclosures. My parents had moved there when I, their only child, had been a mere babe in arms. Mother, a seamstress by profession, and Dad, a store manager, had first met when Mum had gone to Browns Emporium to show her new designs, the very day Dad had been called to the shop floor, to soothe a ruffled customer, and Mum, her arms full of files had problems negotiating the double doors. She had a warm, openly friendly face, with bright green eyes and auburn hair, and he'd found her totally irresistible.

After moving to Cragdale, her work had soon become known, so I grew up in a house frequented by local ladies, and used to seeing them in varying stages of undress, had the advantage, but I never divulged their intimate secrets, not even to my best friend Deirdre Galsworthy, who had passed her exams, like me, for Miss Cramptons High School For Girls, but after leaving to pursue a nursing career in London, and

Deirdre moved to Manchester in her quest to become a librarian, we'd sadly drifted apart. At the onset of the Second War, I'd become a nursing sister, and when Deirdre had been fatally injured in a bombing raid, I'd grieved with her family, and have pangs of remorse ever since. Meanwhile I married my shy, loving, clever scientist husband, whom I adored, and when he's been laid to rest after undergoing two strokes, I'd returned to my roots, and found comfort with those I had grown up with and left behind in my search for knowledge.

It being market day, I'd looked for bargains, with the church bazaar in mind, whilst the numbing effect of the dentist's injection wore off, and when it had, made my way to 'Maud's Pantry', a homely little cafe, with olde worlde charm and excellent food. Mathilda Underwood immediately caught my eye as I entered, and inclining her head, with what passed for a smile, I'd begun weaving my way towards her, only to be side-tracked by John Carter, who, not aware of my intent, asked me to join him. I'd mouthed 'sorry' to Mathilda, but she'd scowled her displeasure, looked as if she might get up and leave, changed her mind, and because I faced her, proceeded to discomfit me, until John said, 'I'm glad you are here, there's something I want your opinion about, before the council meeting,' so whilst I ordered an omelette, and cherry pie to follow, we'd discussed his suggestion about holding the garden fete on the vicarage lawn, and not the proposed village green. He'd made me laugh so much that day, the time had flown, and I couldn't believe how the cafe had emptied when we'd stood up to leave. I had only to call in 'The Pin Cushion', for embroidery silks, but the shades I most wanted were out of stock, and scolding myself for being late, only just managed to catch the train. At Cragdale, Mathilda had left ahead of me, and though I'd stepped out briskly, she had been nowhere in sight, but when I'd apologised after the Sunday service, she's simply ducked her head, given her companion a sly glance, then excused herself without meeting my eye. Then there was John and his attractive wife Amy, so I invited them to lunch. Amy hadn't minded in the least John and I sharing a meal in Bolverton, so I was both hurt and surprised when she snubbed me, and pointedly crossed the street. I can't remember when I first noticed the whispered asides and furtive snide remarks, but when John, in his embarrassment, averted his gaze, and no longer offered a hand when meeting, I recognised mischief afoot, and had no problem guessing who, but as I gradually withdrew from village affairs, no one remarked on my absenteeism, except the vicar, who had called and stayed to tea. 'What's wrong?' he'd asked concernedly. He had an endearing habit of putting just the right inflection in his voice. The sort that brings a lump to one's throat, with an urgent desire to tell all, but I'd refrained, swallowed hard, and explained my suspicions, watched the changing emotions wash over his naturally pale face, the deepening grey of his eyes, the increased vee between them, and felt I had gained a friend, albeit if one out of his depths, and to ease his discomfort, I said, in my experience a catalyst unusually presented itself, only I couldn't know how soon that was to be.

The news, filtering through the grapevine, finally reached me, but too late to offer my help, Mathilda had fallen, breaking her hip, and after lying helpless all night, she'd managed to alert the milkman. Her transference to hospital had been speedily executed, and I must have been the only one not to visit.

On the day of her release, Sally Walker, the district nurse 'popped in', for coffee, and asked if I would be prepared to call on Mathilda.

'You know what you are saying don't you?' I'd said. 'If you haven't heard about my alleged home wrecking, you must be the only one.' She'd laughed then, saying meeting the enemy head on, often brought about peace, so I accepted the challenge, I knew Mathilda's weakness for scones and coconut tarts, and baked that morning. Then, when the ambulance had driven away, I'd cut roses, fern and yellow picatee carnations from the garden, and walked, head high, to the house at the end of the street. My knock had been answered by a much weakened voice, and I've yet to see a smile vanish as quickly as hers.

'Good morning,' I said, 'Nurse asked me to call or I wouldn't have intruded, but now I'm here, how can I help?' so I made a cup of tea, prepared her lunch, arranged the flowers, and helped her to the toilet. She was no lightweight, but determination strengthened my arm, then telling her I would return later, unless I heard otherwise, I let myself out. During the ensuing days I made caring for her my priority, it wasn't easy, but I had nothing to lose, especially as the visitors wearied of calling, until there was just Mathilda and me.

One day, she had begun speaking, tentatively at first, about her family, how lonely life had become, since those, including her husband, were green mounds in the churchyard. I had the distinct impression of her wanting to say more and wished later she had never found the courage to make known, what ought never to have been revealed.

'It was during the war,' she'd begun. 'I wasn't so plain-looking then. My marriage wasn't all I'd hoped, and with Stanley in Italy, I looked elsewhere, and I wasn't alone,' she glowered spitefully. 'We loved each other, and I believe he would return when he received orders to move on, only he didn't, he'd been gone a week or two when I discovered he'd left me a present. I couldn't face staying here, so I told my folks I was off to care for a sick friend in Manchester. I found cheap lodging and worked in munitions, but once the baby showed, I had to leave. After that I worked where I could and a week or so before the end, the baby stopped moving, so it was no surprise when I delivered him stillborn. I saw to myself and nobody was the wiser. Then, under cover of an air-raid, I wrapped him up, stole into the night, and laid him in the ruins of a building.'

In the lengthy silence, I envisaged how it must have been, the horror of what desperation had compelled her to do, wiped out the distress she had inflicted, and as the grandfather clock wheeled asthmatically before striking I crossed the room, put my arms around her and comforted her as she cried herself empty. 'My husband,' she continued, wiping her eyes, 'came back, only he wasn't the one I wanted to see. He always blamed me for being sterile, but all the time it was him, only I couldn't say, and so I bore all the pain and wretchedness like a shroud until his death. I saw you on your return.' Her eyes glinted like burning coals, in her contorted face, 'Saw how everyone flocked round you, hanging onto your every word, and I hated you, hated your youthful looks,' and as she rambled vindictively, I thought of how I must appear to her, for age had not treated me unkindly, and the lines round my brown, widely spaced, long lashed eyes, could be attributed to my ready laughter, whilst my inherited auburn hair, only slightly peppered with grey, frames my face in soft curls, so that I had not been totally dissatisfied with what the mirror revealed.

'No one,' she was saying bitterly, 'gave me so much as a glance, except the children, who merely poked fun.'

'So you couldn't wait to discredit me, by spreading lies.'

'It didn't look like that to me. You were giving him the eye, and he, like everybody else was besotted with you, Amy had a right to know.'

'If it had been true, I couldn't agree more, but we were simply, innocently, enjoying a light-hearted meal. You should not judge before you know the facts. You've made a nonsense of a good marriage. I doubt trust will ever be established, and John will spend the rest of his days wondering how to repair the damage you have done. Even if I go away, the stigma will remain,' and try as I would, I could not keep the anger from my voice.

So here we are, trying to smooth over the cracks, whilst Mathilda lies in the family plot outside the church, having suffered a coronary thrombosis. At least she is at rest. It is we who are left to piece together the shattered remnants and start all over again.